This book is dedicated to
Marilyn, Clark, Humphrey, Linda
and the rest of the gang.

Copyright © 1990 by Thomas G. Tolnay

s reserved. No part of this book may be reproduced or
. in any form or by any means, electronic or mechanical,
otocopying, recording, or by any information storage and
ystem, without permission in writing of the Publisher.
racters and events portrayed in this work are fictitious.
ublished in the United States of America in 1990
by Walker Publishing Company, Inc.
d simultaneously in Canada by Thomas Allen & Son
Canada, Limited, Markham, Ontario
rary of Congress Cataloging-in-Publication Data
Tolnay, Thomas
Celluloid Gangs / Tom Tolnay
ISBN 0-8027-5753-7
I. Title.
PS3570.04285E83 1989
813'.54-dc20   89-16534
CIP

Printed in the United States of America
2 4 6 8 10 9 7 5 3 1

Cellul

Tom

Walke
New

$\triangledown$

1
ABDUCTION SCENE

AN HOUR OF PECKING and staring at the humming Smith-Corona had failed to scare up so much as a lead graph—not one Lejak would print, not even in this rag. Without filing a report on the fire at the pound—fifty-one mutts had perished like . . . like dogs—without looking down Monica's blouse at the switchboard, I walked out of the tabloid's mold-green walls, sank toward ground zero in the shaky elevator, and stood out on West Twenty-ninth wondering what to do with myself. The clogged air was unfit for dog or man, and the sun was running out of juice, spilling shadows into the alleys between the warehouses and factories and office buildings. Soon another day would be down the pipes, and I would still be broke and horny. Only more so.

Toward Second Avenue I dragged this gloomy sense of wasted life, past deadline in so many ways. With a beginning like mine, how could I expect a happy ending? In the land of cannibalized cars where I grew up—better known as the South Bronx—if your garbage can had a lid you were considered upper crust. But if you had no roots you were definitely low-brow, and I was a cultural mess. My father's name and temperament are Spanish, but my mother has the narrow face and mind of a WASP. Good people in their own way, if only because they tried. Yet they never figured out how to live with each other, and after my father disappeared I roamed in the shadows of Yankee Stadium sneered at by the Jews, and scorned by the Puerto Ricans.

By the time I was nineteen I was lugging bundles of racing sheets to newsstands and taking night courses in journalism at Bronx Community. I wanted a better life. Later I worked as a proofreader on a Bronx weekly and did some freelance reporting for *Rubber Tire Dealer*. Both publications folded, and that should've taught me something. But here I was fifteen years later still eating and sleeping among the working poor, just farther down the same subway line in Manhattan, a neighborhood so destitute we have only one kind of bird.

That's how I felt along about then—as small and vulnerable as a sparrow up against the granite cornerstones of New York. And sure enough, at the corner of Third Avenue and East Forty-first, a vintage, six-door Packard limousine, black as the space between stars, eased up to me with a sleek silence. Door number five sprang open, and I found myself nose to nose with a handful of tempered steel.

"Get in," said the long, lavish brunette.

With my luck, nothing surprised me. But the look and sound of the scene—straight out of a forties movie—inspired me to say, "You gotta be kidding." The woman made a believer out of me by cocking the hammer of the howitzer.

I'd hung around outside enough precinct houses to recognize a bona fide .38, especially within gunpowder-burn range. "Yes, ma'am!" I gushed, scrambling into the Packard and closing the door ever so politely. The barrel-backed goon at the steering wheel bashed a button on the dash, and the back door locked automatically with the snap of a rib kicked in.

Suddenly the city seemed miles away.

Even in the pall of her pistol I could appreciate what the

brunette did for a shiny black sheath. The eruptions of her flesh smoothed out every slippery ripple, resolving into glossy swells of sensuality. Mounds of lustrous dark silk were stacked up her skull like the spires of St. Patty's Cathedral. Her purple eyes seemed on the verge of a bright idea. And her lips, jezuz, her lips were the color of orchids and smooth as mink and pulled into a natural, continuous pucker. Looking that good was a violation of the morals code.

"What's this all about?" I ventured.

With a voice as wispy as a scarf stamped in Hong Kong, the pucker said, "Shut up."

I followed orders, sinking back into the plush-as-carpet seat like a very rich brat who has just been collected at a very exclusive private school by a very snobbish mama. That's what I wished were the deal. Actually I was a thirty-eight-year-old, underpaid, overworked, blood-and-guts reporter for the *National Squealer*, a weekly that fed on gore like rats on entrails in a hospital garbage can; a hack scribe who, for some idiotic reason, had been snatched off the concrete by a pair of outmoded mutes. Neither said a word as we rolled away from the curb without so much as a gasp from the carburetor.

"Did I spit on your whitewalls or something?"

"Did you not hear the lady?" growled the driver through the bullet-proof divider. "Unless spoken at, your trap keep shut!"

The beast hulking over the wheel was as perfectly cast as the beauty. Ripples of rubbery skin were bunched up the back of a neck as wide as a fire hydrant; absolutely no hair was visible on him from behind. The patent-leather chauffeur's cap was ridiculously small for the basketball that was balanced where a head should have been. His shoulders were outrageously wide—would've made good outriggers for a crane. Just then he stick-shifted into low, easing the bomber past a parked patrol car. Two cops, a man and a woman, were laughing in the front seat. He must've been playing with the kitty between her legs.

The dame with the gun—somehow I just couldn't help thinking of her as a dame—leaned toward me and squinted, so there wasn't much I could do about the cops. At first I figured it'd finally dawned on this squirrel that she had the wrong nut. But then she hissed, "We know what you were up to the night of February twenty-fifth."

Everything I'd done longer than a week ago ran together like one endless day and night, and the Yankees were already packing up their bats in St. Petersburg to open at the Big Ballyard in the Bronx against the Indians. So I hadn't the faintest clue what I was up to one night last winter. Could've been washing down horse meat with a pitcher of Piels at Danny's Pub; or shaking my fist at the Knicks' being hit and run down by the Detroit Pistons at the Garden; or sitting in the first row of some cold movie house, picking popcorn out of my teeth. The way my deck had been shuffled, I knew one thing for sure: on the night of February twenty-fifth I was not at the Plaza Hotel getting laid.

"What did you do with it?" she continued.

"With what?" I inquired gently, so as not to vibrate her trigger finger.

"Don't play dumb with me."

"I'm not playing dumb. This is the way I was made."

Scraping the sharp edges of her teeth together, she said: "Guess we'll have to refresh your memory."

Getting hit with so many clichés all at once bumped me off the ledge of sanity, I guess, because I went into a streak of crazy chatter. "Easy with that cannon. Those gadgets can make a mess of a man's image. You've got the wrong guy. I was climbing Mount Rushmore that night. Take me to my apartment and I'll show you my birth certificate. My name is—"

"We've already been there."

"To my place? Up on Second Avenue?" It seemed like dirty pool.

"What a peegsty," said the hog up front, and I knew he had the right address.

Instead of being distressed that a couple of strangers had barged into the one corner of the world that was more or less my domain—I was only two months behind on my rent—I got defensive over what they thought of my socks under the bed, and the pile of unwashed dishes in the sink. But it was just as well they didn't swing up toward my room. My birth certificate was at the bottom of a mashed cardboard box in my mother's basement in Teterboro, New Jersey.

Keeping the rod aimed at me, the dame rapped the glass shield with the ruby on her knuckle. "Take us out to The Big House." I distinctly heard the capital *T* and *B* and *H* in her voice.

The driver grunted the way King Kong had the first time he spotted Fay Wray.

The Packard *flump-flump-flump*ed over the steel ribs of the Fifty-ninth Street Bridge. Only a smudge of dried blood was left of daylight in the sky.

"Listen, folks, you're barking up the wrong tree," I said, paying them back with some of their own medicine.

My caretakers didn't bother responding, having settled into the murderous mazes of their minds, and a tune tinkled in my head: "Show me the way to go home, I'm tired and I want to go to bed." Only trouble was that I hadn't had "a little drink about an hour ago," and yet something really had gone to my head. The craft flattened the tar of the ramp with a ruthless momentum. Onto one of the exiting tributaries, past the crumbling industrial lots, the halfhearted factories of Long Island City, we coasted. In the sideview mirror, the dots of green light pinpointing the bridge were draped across the city's throat like the scar of an operation.

Pocked by the glare of streetlights, the boulevard looked like the surface of the moon as it heaved the steel frame of the Packard in great, slow shoulderings. Ten minutes later we stretched up a right-turn embankment and edged in among the slow-rolling, hungry-for-home Fords and Toyotas and VWs, which were fuming on a road someone had been ironical enough to dub the Expressway.

"Lonny's really going to be steamed up," said the lady in black, peering impatiently into the traffic.

The driver shrugged helplessly.

"Be faster to walk," I hinted. No one bit, so I turned my head toward the window and stuck my tongue out at the big-eared family in the car next to us, hoping one of those dumbos behind those slabs of safety glass would realize things weren't kosher in the Packard.

"Keep it up," King Kong growled, glaring at me in the rearview bombsite, "and I peel your face like apple."

Within fifteen minutes we poured down a runway of concrete onto a fluorescent-blue thoroughfare. Here he let those twelve cylinders show off their compression, pulling away from the crowd of wheels, timing the traffic lights brilliantly. I didn't know the Island from Beverly Hills, so I was just as lost on Sunrise Highway as I would've been on Sunset Boulevard. In half an hour we veered right off the double-laner, cruising at a slower, steady speed until the suburban road broke down into a series of unlighted curves and crescents that were lined with the same-sized, evenly spaced, inhabited cigar boxes of Nassau or Suffolk County. The longer we drove, the farther apart the houses were parked, and the closer the trees elbowed each other. Gradually the boxes disappeared altogether, along with the sidewalks. The lack of concrete made me feel more insecure than the cold steel in her hand.

Somewhere on Long Island, not far from where the sand was eroding into the Sound, we were steamrolling over the night: miles beyond Sagamore Hill, Old Westbury, and those other Moneydoms. Wherever we were, it was removed from the traffic of common life, with holdings so vast no one could boast the luxury of neighbors. In the heart of each surveyance, on a knoll, there would be an almost-castle of weathered, white, chiseled stone, surrounded by a rigidly regulated landscape. These establishments were out of human sight from the road. Yet you knew they were there, like the implication of negotiable bonds in the vaulted ceiling of a bank.

"Wonder if there are any vacancies around here," I declared.

"For you there's an opening at Greenlawn Cemetery," the dame replied.

$\triangledown$

2
MUSEUM PIECE

A RUB OF HARD moon polishing its hood into a bottomless black pool, the Packard wafted up to a pair of cylindrical concrete pillars. The two guards were not wearing gray uniforms with billed caps but sharp-snipped suits, pinstriped, plus polka-dot ties. Swinging open the pronged iron gates, the block-shaped one touched the brim of his fedora with an extended finger. We were expected.

Through a winding pattern of professionally pruned, knee-high ornamentals we glided. Massive pines, like hooded members of a satanic sect, spread their caped shadows. Farther up the slope, the first traces of man-generated light fragmented through a confusion of white birch, barely outlining something geometric.

This was no mansion we were rolling toward, the shards of marble crunching like fresh cornflakes beneath our wheels. This was the Metropolitan Museum, give or take a wing. Shaped like an enormous orange crate on its side, it seemed to have been constructed in three installments. The center section was topped by a turret, and someone stood on lookout up there. Spotlights smeared a cold-cream brightness over the concrete facing, which was gouged from decades of exposure to gritty, salty air. The overhang of the roof was decorated with fancy, corroded scrollwork, leading up to a snow-capped mountain hammered out of brass in the center. Although it looked as if the whole thing could be dismantled and stored in a warehouse, I was impressed. Under a high, recently whitewashed portico we pulled up, right behind an immaculately conceived, salmon-enameled Studebaker sedan, a masterwork of the late thirties or early forties. Its fenders were decades ahead of their time, fanning as gracefully as a Rockette's flanks to within inches of the turf. The sedan was another piece in the evening's puzzle. But all I could think about was getting out of there, and I couldn't shake one persistent inconsistency: If they had the wrong guy, how did they know my place was on Second Avenue?

"Move it!" said the brunette, and my kidney jabbed by the steel nozzle, I moved it—out of the Packard and up a tier of steps darkened by unknown thousands of rubber soles.

"There's been a crazy mistake," I said pleasantly.

"Your mistake was being born."

That was one rap, I thought, they couldn't nail on me.

Climbing up the stairs, I realized the deeper I stepped into this thing, the tougher it would be to get away—back to my room-and-a-half walkup, to my army hospital bed and Sherman tank bureau and thirteen-inch portable Admiral. I considered making a run for it. But why risk a couple of slugs in the back with nowhere better to go than that military depot?

King Kong, it turned out, was the size of Tarzan's ape—well, almost as short as me. Except he had clout, pounding thunderously on the freshly stained mahogany door. A set of long, careful limbs in tux and tails swung open the door, saving it from being rapped into two-by-fours. As I was ushered in like the guest of honor, I heard the tux whisper, "Good show," and the dame reply, "Won't be long now." Kong widened an eye at the tux, then headed back down the stairs toward the Packard. Behind me, the door shut with a boom.

Along the broad, hollow, cool corridor were boxed compartments with round and square gadgets cast in black iron, like old-time inventions. Blown-up, dust-dulled photographs of early-in-the-century faces were wired to the walls. Down an Arabesque tiled hall off the main drag I spotted a row of plaster statues done up in faded period costumes—Louis XIV, English World War I aviator, knight in armor, an American Indian and similar characters out of history. Since several of the statues were missing fingers and noses, I figured they must've been worth something. Maybe this place really was a museum.

At an archway through which a Greyhound bus could be wheeled we took a sharp turn; the sense of driving was so strong I nearly made a left-hand signal. We cruised for half a city block, drawing up to a pair of ten-foot-tall, sheet-metaled doors that immediately rolled open for us. They were powered by a worried-looking man in a mourner's suit, complete with white carnation and dandruff on the shoulders. His greased dark hair was raked straight back. He might have been the local undertaker. When he flashed a pair of pointy eyeteeth, I knew he was capable of the most awful atrocities.

"The boss has been *frantic*," said the lead-faced man, backpedaling to make way for me and the dame. Then he fit the doors together snugly, genteelly, as if we were attending a chamber recital.

"Got here fast as we could, Lonny," said the brunette. "Traffic was murder."

"Exactly what I was just thinking about," he whispered. It was hard to tell if he meant traffic or murder.

"Our friend," she said, tilting her head toward me, "isn't being cooperative."

He looked at me as I if I'd dragged my intestines in after me. "If he bats an eye, shoot him."

"That's all I'd have to do!" Her pupils flicked toward the ceiling where, I supposed, the higher-ups were lounging around, exercising the freedom of their power. "A nose job'll take care of him."

Just like the statues, I thought, only I'd be worth a lot less, not more. With my eyes locked open, I checked out my new environment. Four of the five walls—the room came to a point—were stacked with books, floor to ceiling. Who sez nobody reads anymore? Spaced twenty feet apart were two desks rounded and ridged at their corners, an attempt at modernism that dated the furniture squarely in the forties. Each was topped by a few large volumes, some kind of rewinding contraption, and a cloudy porcelain lamp with a shade pieced together from thin shreds of shell. Or were they human fingernails?

The undertaker slipped a mother-of-pearl penknife from his pocket, pried it open, and inserted the blade under his thick thumbnail: either keeping his sensitivities sharpened or letting me know that my nails might soon be added to the lampshade. Glancing at the ketchup stain on my lapel, the hairy man stepped close to me and rasped, "Before I call the boss down here, I think you should know we are going to get the goods from you. It's simply a matter of how. My advice to you, Igor Lopes, is to save yourself a lot of unnecessary anguish."

I had been concentrating so earnestly on his eloquent threat that for a moment it escaped my notice he had pronounced my name correctly—without the Spanish Z, as in "antelopes."

$\triangledown$

3

THE ABOMINABLE BOSS

A HUMAN CONFIGURATION LOOMED at the entrance to the room. Silvery shredded wheat sided his head like chrome fender skirts. At his neck was a perfectly turned Windsor knot the size of a fist. On his feet were chalky white, spotless shoes. He was six-foot-three or -four, and might've broken the scale at the Fulton Fish Market. A formidable accumulation of excess life. Remarkably his limp white suit was too large for him, draped sheetlike over his massive bulk. The sight made unavoidable a comparison with the Abominable Snowman.

With eyes like dart tips he peered at the undertaker, then at the dame.

"Nothing," said Lonny.

Suddenly the boss turned on his hockey-puck heel and cooed extravagantly, "My deah Mr. Lopes, welcome to The Big House."

He, too, pronounced my name correctly. But I didn't feel welcome, and wasn't The Big House a nickname for the state prison?

"My friends call me El Cid. May I call you Igor?"

"I've been called worse."

"I trust you had a comfortable journey."

13

His cordiality, punctuated by a comical raising of inky brows, made me feel less threatened. "Your Packard rides as smooth as a good screw. I didn't realize the Smithsonian rents out from its collection."

Though trying not to show it, the boss seemed slightly impatient with me. "I've been most anxious to meet you."

"Sorry I can't say the same," I replied, immediately biting my tongue.

"Quite all right, sir. I have a feeling we shall be getting to know each other considerably better in no time a-tall." His voice sounded as if it were coming up out of a deep ravine.

Despite his toothy smile, I pegged his prediction as hazardous to my health. But I was determined to promote a civilized atmosphere. "Nice layout you got here."

"It is being restored to its former glory."

"With a lodge this size, you'll be painting 'til doomsday."

"For this task we have all the time in the world," he said. "In another matter, however, I'm afraid we have very little of that precious commodity. Nevertheless, I don't believe in conducting business without the proper amenities." At which point he cleared his throat in the direction of his cohorts.

Lonny and the girl sprang to the pointed end of the room, where they swung open a bar cabinet that had been concealed behind a row of false shelves. It was almost as if they were responding to the word of God. It wasn't merely his Abominable's size that commanded respect. It was his style. If this behemoth had been yanking molars out with pliers, you had the feeling he would've done it with class.

"What's your poison?" Lonny wheezed in my direction.

"Anything wet and wild."

"Boss?" said the brunette.

"A drop of cognac, Linda, if you please."

So she had a name.

The undertaker poured for the boss and me, not for himself and the brunette, who, bless her gorgeous black heart, carried the drinks to us without spilling any. I was so grateful for a chance to begin my escape—into the bottle if not into the world—that I swallowed a mouthful without thinking it might've been doctored. It tasted hard as bootleg booze, but at least my brain didn't go numb. Not any more than usual. Seems they required my presence of mind for the time being. Good. I wanted to see what was going to be done with me.

"Here's to your continued good health, sir," said El Cid, downing his glass of lighter fluid in one masterful gulp. "Aaah. That's better," he said, waving me toward a chair.

That's a start was how I felt about the matter, taking another swallow before sinking onto a chair that was heavy as barroom furniture. The Abominable Boss squeezed into its matching mate five feet away, and the glue cracked in its joints.

"Do you indulge?" he asked, drawing a cigar out of his inside pocket.

"I kicked the habit," I said, wondering why the fat cat was coming on as palsy walsy as a gym teacher who had put aside his brutality for open-school week.

The boss bit off the tapered end of the tightly rolled black cigar and apparently swallowed the stub. Pinching a tiny match with his stubby fingers out of a little wooden box, he somehow managed to light up. "Igor," he said amidst a pearly puff, "my colleagues are under the impression you are unsympathetic to our cause."

"I tried to tell your pals, but they wouldn't listen. You've got the wrong bird."

"No, no, Igor. You are the man—or bird, as you say—that we need. No one else will do."

Shaking my head, I muttered, "I don't even know what you want."

As he sat there disbelieving me, I noticed that Linda had set the .38 down on the corner of the desk to light a cigarette. Puffed up by the taste of booze, I pushed my body out of the chair and took a swipe at the gun. But Lonny sprang at me like a wolf on a lamb chop and planted his fist in my ribs, stopping me short.

"Where d'ya think you're goin', buddy?"

Blood rushed out of my brain down to where it was needed more. The light thickened, making it difficult to see. Breathing wasn't too easy either. Suspecting his question had been rhetorical, I didn't bother replying.

The undertaker shoved me back into the chair, his teeth gleaming, and he growled at Linda, "Don't be so careless, dammit."

"Even if he'd gotten the gun," she said defiantly, "what could he have done with it anyway?"

Linda didn't think much of me. Too bad. I was ready to fall in love with her with no more encouragement than a kind word.

"That was a very foolhardy thing to do, Igor," El Cid said, his face red with annoyance. "I prefer to ease into business. Now you have forced me to be entirely too direct." He took a heavy breath. "We want the film you took from Mr. Goldwine's mansion, and we want it without delay."

Well, well, well. It was for a strip of celluloid that I was being dented. "You mean the big-shot producer who was bumped off?" I gasped, rubbing my ribs gingerly.

"February twenty-fifth to be precise."

Just like that I remembered what I was doing the night of the twenty-fifth. I happened to be hanging out around the emergency ward of New York Hospital—where there's blood there's a story—just as the call came in from the butler.

Goldwine must've still been alive at that point; otherwise he would've called the police first. Out of the hospital I'd bounced and into the street, using my fake limp to shame a cabbie into stopping for me. Soon we were bumping along behind the ambulance.

Goldwine's fortress turned up on Fifth Avenue, overlording Central Park; it was the only building on the block that could afford to be less than ten stories tall. The blocks of banker's granite made me feel like writing up a withdrawal slip. In the confusion I was able to pop in on the heels of the fags in white coats, and I poked around under the high ceilings of his chambers. The medics and butler thought I was a city dick, which was understandable since I had flashed a phony ID. Actually, I was just an everyday schmuck who was too nosy for his own health. And me without my major medical paid up. But Goldwine was out of the running by the time I got there. He looked more like fifty pounds of chopped meat than two hundred pounds of movie mogul. It took a lot of bullets, or one well-placed .45, to make a mess like that.

"That was a weird case," I said to El Cid. "The butler insisted he hadn't let anyone in or out of the house all night. And after he went to his room, he heard a crash, but no gunshots. Later the police couldn't find any signs of a break-in. Even though things pointed to the butler, the cops couldn't pin anything on him—insufficient evidence, plus no motive. The butler had been with him for years and was loyal—even protective—toward his employer. To complicate matters, the old boy had a stroke and died within weeks of the murder." Suddenly I realized I was doing that crazy chatter again.

The boss exposed startlingly long incisors. "I read your accounts of the affair with considerable interest."

It was nice to know someone actually read that rag, but the *News* had done the best stories on the killing, and I said so.

"I'm not referring to journalistic style so much as timing." El Cid grimaced. "The other papers didn't get there 'til much later."

Just then a signal was sent to my brain by the rock-bottom tones of the Abominable Boss's voice, by the folds of his powdery-white skin, but I couldn't quite pick it up. "So what?"

Lonny cracked his knuckles, as if asking the boss for permission to break my hands.

"As you undoubtedly know, Igor," El Cid said with the daintiness of the ballet-dancing elephant in *Fantasia*, "the motion picture in your possession was never released to the public because of a legal battle involving compensation arrangements for actors on loan from other companies. For years my colleagues and I searched the globe for it—quite fruitlessly. Finally I began to accept that the masterprint— the only copy extant—had been lost forever. Not long before Mr. Goldwine's unfortunate demise, however, we discovered that the film was still catalogued as part of his private collection. And I could not get out of my mind the thought that a man with his genius for detail would not have continued to list the film—not unless *Escape to Monte Carlo* did indeed still exist."

Escape to Monte Carlo. That's what I wanted to do. "None of this has anything to do with me."

Flicking his ashes and grinding them into the rug, El Cid said with a rising voice, "You persist in maintaining your ignorance in this matter. Interesting. But inconsistent with the facts. We have made a thorough inspection of Mr. Goldwine's residences in New York and Hollywood and

Palm Beach. And it was clear from the transcript of the hearings, and from our own contacts with the butler and hospital attendants, that they knew nothing of the film. Then I remembered seeing the headlines—the exclusives— on the case in the *National Squealer*. We got ahold of the back issues, and it became quite evident, sir, that you were the only other person who had an opportunity to go through his rooms before the police arrived."

The passion with which he delivered this speech made me curious. "What's so important about the film, anyway?"

As if suddenly aware of his own zeal, El Cid spoke carefully and quietly. "The film has a certain . . .historical significance to the members of our Cultural Alliance."

"If it's only history you're after, why's everybody getting so uptight?"

El Cid looked at me grimly but maintained his composure. "It's not simply history, my good man; it's irretrievable history. Many early films have been endangered due to the deterioration of the celluloid on which they were recorded. With a film that has been exposed to extraordinary heat, light, dust—or all three, this process of decay is greatly accelerated. And if there are no other copies, the talents, labors, and ideas of dozens of people—not to mention a multitude of greenbacks—would be washed away like . . . like—"

"Yeah, I know, like footprints in the sand."

"Precisely. Modern transfer techniques and materials have enabled the industry to preserve many important films. But only if the restoration is effected in time."

"That's a sad story, a very sad story."

"For all we know," said El Cid, by now speaking mostly to himself, "the fate of *Escape to Monte Carlo* may already have been sealed by time."

Staring at the knoll that was his midsection, I could feel that signal trying to penetrate the sludge of my mind again. Just then I realized we were not surrounded by books. The shelves were lined with inch-wide, colored cartons that contained film reels—thousands of motion pictures. The room was a film library, a repository of lovers and pirates and monsters and cowboys and gangsters and comedians and ghosts on celluloid, a material that was apparently falling apart even as we spoke.

"Each day, each hour becomes more critical," he said thickly. "Now do you understand why we must insist upon your immediate cooperation?"

Despite my strong instinct for self-preservation, the caper was beginning to raise my curiosity, along with a hearty slice of American greed. "What do you suppose such a rare film might be worth?"

"The value of the film is essentially cultural," he said, the word "value" rolling off his tongue like a gold coin off the fingers. "Nevertheless, we would make a certain honorarium available to you."

"Couldn't you get a little more specific?" I wanted to hear numbers ring in the cash register between my ears.

"The Alliance is prepared to make available to you a sum of . . .twenty-five thousand dollars."

"These days right-fielders who hit under .250 make a million bucks."

"You must understand that The Big House is a nonprofit organization."

"Why don't you apply for a government grant?"

El Cid glanced at his sidekicks ominously, and I realized my greed was getting me deeper into trouble. "I never actually *said* I have it."

"Please, Igor," said El Cid sadly, "there is no time for

fox-trotting. Your articles made it perfectly clear you had access to Mr. Goldwine's personal possessions."

"The cops showed up and threw me out."

In a voice that sounded like shrapnel hitting water, Linda sizzled, "You were inside a good twenty minutes before they showed up, you crumb."

El Cid held up his hand to her and said to me, "Mr. Goldwine was too committed to film to have destroyed or parted with it—not willingly. Yet the film was not among his effects following his untimely death. Only the butler and Igor Lopes had the opportunity to roam freely about the Goldwine quarters before the police arrived. The butler's story has been checked out thoroughly. That leaves you."

"Wait a minute. You're forgetting the murderer."

"We've been all over that ground as well. No, Igor, it had to be you."

I gazed out the tall, narrow window. Over me like an eclipse fell a longing to be out in that white moonlight, playing roamin' hands and rushin' fingers with Maryjane Schnapper on the roof of our old tenement in the Bronx. Had I married her upon graduation from South Bronx High, as threatened, I wouldn't have been in this fix.

"Probably the cops got their hooks into it," I suggested vaguely.

"They would not have recognized its significance, so it would have remained with his effects."

"How about the executors of Goldwine's estate? Didn't they have to go around putting labels on everything?"

"You were there before them, and so were we."

"What makes you think I'd have known the film was worth something?"

"Well, now, that's an intriguing question. And I'm not entirely sure of the answer. Perhaps in searching for details

for your articles you came across one of the letters referring
to *Monte Carlo*—its uniqueness, its fate—and so you cross-
referenced it with the catalog."

"If you couldn't find it with all your efforts, I don't know
why you imagine I would've found it."

"I suspect you got lucky and found it lying out on a shelf
after a recent private screening. Or perhaps you stumbled
upon a secret hiding place that Mr. Goldwine kept for films
that were one of a kind. After that, you either took the film
with you or put it back into its hiding place. Only you can
say for sure what really happened that night."

"I told you what happened, but you won't listen."

"Igor, I think I should warn you that I have a deadly
temper." And I could see he was working hard to hold it in.

"If I had it, believe me I would sell it to you right
away—my rent is overdue."

"Not if you had a better offer."

Now, what the hell was that supposed to mean?

To put an end to this jabber, maybe all I had to do was
develop a case of lockjaw. What could I lose, except a few
teeth? And I still had plenty of those left. So I stared at a
dark dot on Abominable's left shoulder—probably a fly
resting its wings during the long trip up to his head. And
when he fired several questions at me, such as "Where do
you have it hidden?" and finally, "For the last time, are you
going to cooperate?", I did not say a word. I just stared at
the fly, which now took off and landed on the tip of his nose.
But he was so self-possessed he didn't even blink or bother
to brush it away.

The boss, aiming his eyes like gun barrels into mine,
enunciated, "Linda, *si'l vous plait*," and an unyielding object
sank half an inch into the back of my skull. A real sweetheart

this chick is, I thought as I twirled away from awareness like a maple seed off the mother branch. But it could've been a lot worse. This charming product of finishing-off school could just as coldly have emptied the contents of that short-nosed dehumanizer into my vitals. Instead of loosening my tongue, though, the crack on the cranium slid me out of the chair in slow motion, and I landed softly in a reverie that flickered in my mind like a silent movie.

I was at Goldwine's New York mansion the night of the murder, trying to bust past actor Wallace Beery, who was playing the butler. Luckily, I got my neck out the door in time before he slammed it shut. Around to the back of the institution I dashed, where I wiped the gold dust off the long-paned window, and peered in. Little round Goldwine and big square El Cid were bellowing like wild boars in heat. The boss cried out, "If we don't obtain that film immediately, we will be doomed!" And Goldwine moaned, "*Escape to Monte Carlo* was destroyed in a studio fire years ago." To which El Cid replied, "Then why is it still listed in the inventory of your collection?" Before Goldwine could respond I heard five evenly timed blasts come from the top of the stairs, but I didn't see anyone up there. All I saw was the crimson spreading out from the center of Goldwine's gray silk robe like a bunch of bright roses blooming in time-lapse photography. . . .

Just like that I was back in the library on Long Island. The boss was breathing cigar clouds into my bloodless face, and the fly on his nose was gone. Now I could hear him faintly, as though from a long way off . . . "Unless you come across, it's curtains for you."

"Spare me the clichés," I said, or at least thought, not having entirely crossed the divide of consciousness. In that smoky stupor, gazing up his hairy nostrils, it seemed to me that El Cid was not a human being at all. He seemed more like a symbol, an image. And a moment before my grip on the world gave way again, his sounds and features funneled down to a comprehensible whole, into a name: Sydney Greenstreet.

4
GHOSTS GALORE

THE KNOB ON MY cranium was control central for an intense, persistent impulse that seemed to electrocute my brain with each throb: shocks I figured were the last strokes of life escaping my nervous system. Then I noticed a narrow streak of brightness, low, expanding and contracting off to my left in time with the throb. Another streak sliced above what I had begun to realize was a door. . . . I hadn't gotten off that easy.

Now I remembered—Sydney Greenstreet! So it wasn't El Cid, but El Syd. All the other faces of the evening began to come together with names that had been rumbling beneath my consciousness like the A train under Eighth Avenue. The Undertaker was Lon Chaney, Jr., the Butler was Arthur Treacher, the Driver was Eric von Stroheim, and the Dame . . . the Dame was Linda Darnell! But the throb in my skull was too distinct for a two-dimensional world.

They had hauled me into one of the upper chambers to let me sleep off the butt of Linda's pistol, and I wondered how someone so beautiful could be so heavy-handed. Even more disturbing was the question of time. How could someone so old be so beautiful? Darnell had charmed the cameras in the forties. If Chaney was still around, he should've been sipping tea in a wheelchair. And Greenstreet—Christ, with all that cholesterol, he had to be stretched out under two yards of dirt.

Clips from their movies flashed on my inner screen: Greenstreet ordering one of his flunkies to keep an eye peeled for Claude Rains . . .Chaney wringing his hands with anguish as he returns from the woods beneath a full moon with blood under his fingernails . . .von Stroheim wheeling Gloria Swanson and William Holden down Sunset Boulevard in the bullet-proof touring car . . .Darnell dancing with one man while checking out Paul Douglas, who is drinking at a table with Jeannie Crane. . . . I was amazed at how vivid, how real those experiences seemed to me, even though they were only smoke on strips of celluloid. But why hadn't their names popped into my head sooner? Near as I could figure, it was because my mind couldn't adapt to the idea of a bunch of old-time movie actors kidnapping me.

Hoisting myself up to a sitting position, I found they hadn't even removed my shoes, and there were no sheets on the mattress. Just like home. Slivers of light were piercing the floor through the blinds. I was surrounded by stacks of mattresses and assorted bed frames and posts and headboards. Typical of my luck: wall-to-wall beds, and no broads. Sort of like dying of thirst on an ocean cruise.

Carefully I lugged my head to the window and eased open the wooden blinds. Through a paddy wagon-style grating I saw, maybe fifty feet below, the misty smolder left behind by the moon (or was it the sun coming up?) over a lawn the size of the outfield at Yankee Stadium. Along a knoll of bluish grass I spotted a few couples strolling arm-in-arm, their hair shiny in the leaden light.

From behind me I heard, "The grounds are being reseeded as part of the rehabilitation program."

Jerking around, I discovered my host, his chunky hand strangling the bedpost so he wouldn't topple over and fall through the floor.

"I would hope you are now predisposed to be more accommodating," Sydney said in his inimitable way of sounding slightly superior to his surroundings.

"My head hurts."

"A most regrettable course of action on our part, but entirely justified, I fear."

In spite of myself, I imitated his accent. "Is it morning or is it night?"

"The choice is yours, my good fellow. Transfer the film into my hands and it is endless morning. Withhold the film and it is night—never-ending night."

I wondered if he'd stolen those lines from a movie. "Look, I don't have the film, and I have to go home and put some milk in a saucer for my cat."

"You will be staying on as a house guest," he announced, nodding as if agreeing with himself.

Sydney Greenstreet was no hallucination. He stood there before me, and yet I knew with equal conviction that Sydney Greenstreet had to be long gone. It was beginning to look as though all those movies I'd watched over the years were finally catching up to me, loading down my brain until it was out of kilter. Roaming between the stacks of mattresses, closer to the Abominable Boss, I said, "I'm a working man. If I don't get in by 9 A.M. my editor will come looking for me. And when he finds me, I'll be sent back to the obit department—as an entry."

"I have taken the liberty of ordering a *petit déjeuner* up to your room."

"Spare the toast. I don't have much of an appetite these days."

"If only I could say the same."

"Too many banana splits lately?" I said viciously.

With a crack in his voice, Sydney Greenstreet unexpectedly exposed the underbelly of his tough act: "Had I been less indulgent *au table* over the years, I might not have been cast as a menace but as a leading man. More than one agent assured me I had that potential."

"I used to be a beautiful baby too," I consoled, but he was listening only to himself.

"Indeed, if my career had taken another turn, I would not be in my current predicament."

"Same here."

I thought I saw a gleam of liquid in his frying pan of an eye, and for one thin moment I actually felt sorry for the big slob—the way I'd felt when the other elephants laughed at Dumbo. But he pulled himself together, and as he turned to leave, he spoke over an iceberg of a shoulder, "The subbasement of The Big House contains a complete working replica of a medieval torture chamber. Left over from Vincent Price's wax museum film. The human genius for causing pain is limitless, as you shall see."

In my mind I could see a bed of spikes punctuating my rib cage, and I shuddered.

With my ear against the door I could hear the guard slapping down the cards, probably cheating himself at solitaire. I checked the rest of the long rectangular room for a way out, but there was only the grated window, and I was a long way up. Finally I sat down on a mattress and thought about God awhile, wondering if He was too busy to help someone in distress. Particularly an accomplished sinner like me.

Not much later the door unbolted with a sound that could've served as a sound effect for a body hitting the floor. In came a character wearing a white silk tie and a navy blue, gabardine suit, followed by the bruiser who must've been guarding my door. The name that went with the gent in the suit—his face was crumpled like a Dixie cup—was floating somewhere in my mind, but I couldn't quite get ahold of it. A black medical bag was in his right hook. The bare-armed, muscle-bound guard in the leather vest looked familiar too. A dagger was tucked in his wide belt. Trouble, I was beginning to think, came in pairs.

"What do you have in mind?" I said to the doc.

The question is, "What do you have in *your* mind?" he said, unfolding his instrument case. Out of its black gape came a long, very long hypodermic needle. And before I had a chance to shrink in horror, I got zapped—"Owwwww! What the hell are you doing, drilling for oil?" I cried, squeezing the sore spot, which showed no sign of blood. But I knew he'd pumped me full of truth serum. Soon I'd be spitting out the secrets of my life, and at that particular moment I wasn't sure I wanted them to know the whole story—their uncertainty was my insurance policy. My lights went out anyway.

In the boob tube in my head Igor Lopes and Linda Darnell were elevatoring up to the Plaza Hotel's elegant bridal suite, in the penthouse, with ankle-deep red rugs, and foot-long gold tassels dripping from the walls. I could see the red half dollars of her nipples through the transparent platinum gown. Her dark satin hair was swirled like a typhoon to one side.

I moved up to her in my ratty yellow terry-cloth robe; I slid the thin straps off her shoulders. The platinum slithered into quicksilver on the floor at her feet. Breathlessly I beheld the unobstructed dips and dimples of God's creative genius before me. Tearing at my robe, I couldn't get the belt untied—no matter how hard I yanked, it wouldn't come undone. . . .

When I came to, my playmates were gone. It seemed I was

spending more time unconscious than conscious, and now, in addition to my head, my arm hurt. But what really bothered me was not knowing what I'd said to them.

I tried the doorknob to see if someone had gotten careless. No dice. And with my guardian angel still playing solitaire outside the door, it wouldn't have mattered much.

Maybe the *Squealer*'s editor would send our rewrite man Ferdy up to my place to drag my ass out of bed—"Hangover or no hangover," and would get curious when I turned up missing. Maybe they would send the cops looking for me. One thing I noticed about being left alone, you start thinking the impossible is possible.

About the time I was revving up for a mental breakdown, the door unbolted and in popped a lean loser, all in gray, with a well-forked pompadour and a look of continuous surprise. Fussily he settled a tray of dishes on a stack of mattresses near the door. This time the guard didn't bother coming in. Another one I hadn't impressed very much.

"I saw this movie," I crowed. "You've poisoned the food just enough to make me sick, right? And then I'll have to come across to get you to give me the antidote to save my life, right?"

"Don't be absurd!"

Soon as I heard that voice I knew that what my eyes had been telling me was true. It was Edward Everett Horton. The place was crawling with movie characters from a widening range of periods—the thirties, forties, fifties, and sixties. Maybe all this wasn't the result of too much movie-gazing. Maybe it was because I'd been working hard as an ant, mixing it with plenty of studious drinking, and the combination had kept me from getting my clutches on a woman in . . . months? . . . years? Nothing'll make you hallucinate more vividly than no screwing.

"Good afternoon," Edward Everett said politely, eyes lowered, heading for the door.

I was hoping some word, some gesture would tip me off on what they had found out. But his eyes and mouth held on to that patented quizzical look of his.

"Now that Syd's found out everything he wanted to know, I guess it won't be necessary to keep me caged up."

"Oh, they couldn't find a thing in your mind. You'll be going down to the torture chamber presently," he said cheerfully.

It occurred to me this was one wimp I could take, so I rushed him, but he hopped quick as Brer Rabbit to the door and grabbed the knob. I stopped dead. "Wait, just do me one little favor. Tell me your name, will you?" I just wanted to hear it from his own lips. Horton laid one of his bemused winces on me and stepped out of the room. I saw the size-46 vest sitting at the folding table, slapping down a card. He looked up at me meanly—I guess he was losing. The door slammed shut and was bolted.

I circled the food a moment, then picked up the fork and stirred the string beans around on the plate: they were green, but I still didn't trust them. Now I leaned close to the plate and sniffed the pork chop. Fried in butter. What the hell, I thought, grabbing hold of the bone and taking a bite.

Not enough salt and pepper. My guts tightened, but I didn't drop dead. Taking that as a reasonably positive sign, I sipped from the transparent cup of java. It tasted bitter, at least a week old. Now I broke into the baked potato, wondering if I should order up some sour cream from room service. But inside the skin I found a folded piece of brown paper, and there was writing on it: "I will come to you tonight. M."   M?

$\triangledown$

5

BLIND DATE

THE SERUM MUST'VE STILL been working on me, because
I felt drowsy all afternoon, and when I lay back to shake off
the sluggishness my mind slid away like a body buried at
sea, one that wouldn't sink completely, dipping in and out
of the laps of sleep. During one stretch of awareness I heard
something edging in and around the mattresses. As tense as
a set mouse trap I lay, but my visitor was too large to be a
mouse. In the dusty light shredding through the window
slats, through the slit between my lids, I saw her—sweet
jezuz—the goddess of love—Miss MM herself. The explo-
sion of blondness made me swoon.

Pinned up in a low-cut, spaghetti-strap white dress, she
leaned down and rested her cleavage on the mattress. What
a load to have to carry around all day. I knuckled my eyes,
but when I looked again Marilyn Monroe was still there.
This was one chick I knew for a fact had croaked. Talk about
the miracles performed by Hollywood makeup artists.

"Speak quietly," she said into my ear, brushing my lobe with
her fleshy lip. A nerve broke loose at the roots of my hair and
wormed all the way down to my toes. It was definitely the
Monroe larynx at work, a voice that sounded as if it had a
dimple built into it.

"Could I have your autograph?"

She looked at me as if I were stoned.

"If you don't have a pen, you can do it in lipstick on my chest."

"*Please.* I need your help."

"You need *my* help?"

"I'm a prisoner too," she said.

"Of love?"

"Of The Big House."

"You're not coming through."

"I know too much."

It was that classic line—a favorite of mine—and served up as if for the first time in the history of movies. But there was no avoiding the fact. It was another whopper of a cliché, a line with such an impressive track record it made me draw in my horns. Her coming up here had to be a setup, and the best way to protect myself was to play along with them.

"How could Igor Lopes possibly help Marilyn Monroe?"

"It'll take beauty *and* brawn to get out of here."

I wondered which I was supposed to supply.

"Once we've picked up the film," she whispered, "they won't be able to push us around. I know some people who'd be willing to cough up a bundle for the film, and we could take off like . . .like . . ."

"Like bats out of hell."

"That's right." She grinned.

Ouch! I thought, but I was beginning to understand why they kept firing clichés at me. To be successful in the movies, each of them had to become a cliché—the sex symbol, the tough guy, the girl next door, the war hero. Movie stars were nothing but a bunch of clichés that made us feel secure because we knew we could count on them to behave in a particular way.

* * *

A key was inserted in the door! Marilyn grabbed a moth-eaten quilt, slid onto the mattress, moved up against me, and we shook the padded cloth out over us. Someone opened the door, wedging an angle of light over the floor. We lay absolutely still, not making a sound. After a couple of seconds, the door closed and was locked. Carefully I peeked out, making sure no one had stayed inside.

Then it hit me—I'm in the sack with Marilyn Monroe! If only Ferdy Bagatelle at the *Squealer* could see me now. Far as I was concerned, Marilyn could've stayed right there forever, flattening the curls on my chest. But good deals never last, not when you hail from the South Bronx. Backing off, she whispered, "What kind of name is Igor Lopes?"

"I was named after Dr. Frankenstein's hunchback helper."

Marilyn giggled softly, but I'd been dead serious. My father had seen the original movie twenty or thirty times before he took off, and was probably still watching it on late-night TV somewhere or other.

When she sat up, I reached up and pulled the zipper on her dress down her back, exposing a set of prime ribs.

Pushing my hand away, she said, "It's the wrong time and the wrong place, Iggy."

I felt like a kid who got left off the neighborhood baseball team. Of course, it was not me, Igor Lopes, she wanted—it was the film. I had to remind myself that her given name was Norma Jean. Hell, she was only a figment of Hollywood's imagination, nothing more than a shadow of the fresh personality and pretty face she had been.

Seeing I felt rejected, I guess, and not wanting to shut me off completely, Marilyn leaned over me and placed her slick lips on my mouth. It was a steady and sweet imprint, one of those kisses men had traded in their children for.

Crumbling immediately, I pleaded, "How'd you like to go to Monte Carlo with me?" If you're going to lie, you might as well lie big.

"Is that where you have the film stashed?"

Since she was leading me on, why couldn't I do the same?—just long enough to end the sex drought I'd been undergoing like an interminable case of flu. "Could be."

"Come on, Iggy," she said, "don't hold out on me."

"Right now I've got other things on my mind."

Marilyn looked down at the bump in my pants and said, "You certainly *do* have something, but it's not on your mind." Just like that, she grabbed ahold of my pecker.

My breathing became as thick as the breeze on a summer night along Forty-second Street when the human steam rises out of the massage parlors and mixes with the humidity. And then it happened—the unspeakable, the unthinkable, even to a man in my condition. She had squeezed too hard, and the sensitive muscles convulsed and pop went my weasel.

"Oh, my God," I said, looking away from her.

"Just as well," she said.

It was not just as well. It was much worse. Now I wanted her all the more, and a large pain started cranking up in my groin. I had to get full relief or I was going to disintegrate.

"Let's get out of here and get the film," Marilyn said.

"Wait!" I moaned, my nuts in knots. "Don't got away. Not now." I stared at my crotch with pity.

"You're just playing with my emotions." Actual tears snaked down her face.

I'd heard her sing that tune before, but I couldn't remember the name of the movie. Then she swung her legs off the side of the mattress like she was getting ready to jump off the *Titanic*.

"Stay in bed with me a while longer and I'll tell you where it is."

"Tell me first."

"Will you stay in bed?"

"Maybe," she said, glancing toward the door.

"Well, it's still in Goldwine's place on Fifth Avenue."

"There's twenty-five rooms in that old mansion."

"And I'll show you which room it's in—afterward."

Before I could do anything about it, she zipped up the back of her dress and hopped off the bed. The tears had dried.

"Get your shoes on," she ordered. "There's no time to waste."

The knob on my head started throbbing again, and I pressed my face into the mattress. Why me? Why me? Why me? After I was finished feeling sorry for myself, I looked up and she was gone. Only, I hadn't heard a door close.

In my crumpled trousers and shirt I sat still a moment, stunned, weighed down by the realization that life had done a number on me again. I had been flesh to flesh with a movie goddess—or a reasonable simulation of one—when, without warning, they had lowered the lights on me, dimmed me out of the picture the way they always did in the romantic scenes of those post-wartime flicks.

$\triangledown$

6
TORTURE CHAMBER

THE GRATING HAD BEEN swung open and Marilyn was
crouched outside the window—a long way above the rhodo-
dendrons on a ledge no wider than a first baseman's mitt.
Now she was wearing one of those silly little veiled hats with
a couple of turkey feathers sticking out the side.

"Right this way!" she said, her tits billowing. "We're going
to climb into the next room."

"If you think I'm going out there," I informed her, crossing
my arms like a roadblock, "you're on speed."

Her knuckles white as she gripped the grating, she drawled
with that delicious brand of seriousness, "How tall are you?"

"What a crazy question at a time like this." I was too
embarrassed to tell her.

"You're going to be a lot taller after they stretch out your
body on that rack in the dungeon."

Being taller didn't sound like such a bad idea, but I liked
pain even less than being short. Muttering to myself, I climbed
up on the sill and eased myself onto the ledge. Not until I was
out there beside her could I appreciate just how high and wide
that museum was, and I repented not having gone to church
more often. To be on the safe side, I bounced a quickie prayer
off the clouds, and the reply was instantaneous: my foot

slipped off the edge—I clawed onto the grating. Now I knew
how Harold Lloyd had felt hanging from the hands of a giant
clock in that silent flick.

"Just don't look down," Marilyn said, moving along the ledge.
Naturally that made me go ahead and do it, causing me
to teeter again. Quickly regaining my balance, I groaned, "I
was better off locked up in the room."

"Only another twenty feet," she said, continuing to inch
along in spiked heels.

With nothing better to do as I millimetered to my left, I
worried that they would spot us from the ground and start
taking potshots at us. But Marilyn climbed into the next
room and I reached the window without drawing fire. MM
grabbed on to my calves, startling me into a backward sway.

She speared my hand. "I've got ya!"

My life was literally in her hands. I leaned down and
jumped in. Though no longer a candidate to flatten the
flower bed below, I went into a fit of trembling.

The room was crowded with tables: square, round, rectangular—nothing but tables stacked from one wall to the other,
just as the other room had nothing but beds. I couldn't figure
out if this was a Salvation Army warehouse or if I was caught
up in a realm in which specialization had reached a very high
level of development.

"Out that door to the left is a staircase," she cooed,
sounding like an elementary-school teacher giving fire-drill
instructions. "We've got to get to those stairs without being
seen by Weissmuller."

So that's who'd been playing solitaire outside the door. I
hadn't recognized Tarzan with clothes on. Having seen him
tear the jaws of a crocodile apart, however, I said, "Let's talk
this over before doing anything rash."

"This may be our only chance to get out of here. Syd's left the grounds, and most of the others are out on the front lawn showing off their scrapbooks to each other. Soon they'll start drifting back to watch old movies."

"Scrapbooks?"

"Their clippings of reviews and mentions in gossip columns."

Marilyn heard or sensed something and twisted toward the door. As she listened, I scanned the curves of her body. She looked like a stuffed panda waiting to be cuddled, and I took one giant step toward her with the idea of giving her a bear hug. "How about one little kiss?"

She backed off. "Syd'll be back from the lab any minute."

I was crushed, but didn't want to show it. "What's he doing, shopping for another guinea pig?"

"Not that kind of lab, silly. He's getting things set up in case they nail down the lost film. First he'll screen it to see what kind of condition it's in; then he'll have the lab techs make quick repairs if necessary. Later on, they'll need to transfer it onto new stock. But time's running out for them."

I didn't understand a word of it, or much of anything else. "What's the idea of all these tables in here, and all those beds next door?"

"These are prop rooms."

I was going to ask her the next logical question about the prop rooms, but she started cooing again.

"Soon as I'm out the door, count to three and head down the stairs—fast."

Without waiting to hear my arguments, Marilyn moved through the maze of tables toward the door. I had no choice but to follow her. Quietly she opened the door and peeked outside. I wondered again if I were being set up.

Monroe flung herself out the door and cut left. I counted to ten—twice. When no lead started flying, I dashed out on tiptoes, too afraid to look back, and made it around the corner without bleeding on the carpet.

Down the long curved staircase, two steps at a time I hoofed, until I tripped and skidded down the last four. Marilyn was waiting for me at the bottom. "Shhhh!" she warned, glancing back up the stairs before pushing through a swinging door.

In one leap we went down three steps into a pantry the width and length of a bowling lane. I landed like a bomb, and she landed like a feather. At the end it opened into a huge kitchen, with battered tin pots and pans hanging from the meat hooks. We passed an icebox that could've accommodated an entire cow. Despite all the culinary hardware, there wasn't a sign of food anywhere. Nor any chefs or busboys. Something smelled fishy.

The high-and-mighty door was blank, giving no warning of the time warp about to suck us in. Out in the heart of the building we stood, at its essence—a huge, damp, moldy, gray space that extended from the bottom to the top of the entire museum, maybe a hundred feet high. Monroe continued scuttling along; I stalled and stared at the spotlights, encrusted with decades of dirt. Great webs that had thickened, or nets that had worn thin, spanned large sections of the iron crossbeams, which supported the roof above and the floating partitions below. Dozens of dry, warped planks were laid out as if the carpenters had left them in the middle of constructing a platform a long time ago. Heavy ropes hung like dead jungle snakes left to dry. Faded canvas backdrops— a bank teller's window, a Parisienne café, a white-fenced-in garden, an amusement-park fairway, a western saloon, and who knows how many other fake fronts—were peeling against the walls, like the times and places they represented. In a corner of the stone floor was a scatter of paper reels, the kind they used to store silent movies on.

Suddenly it hit me. This must be the original silent-movie studios I'd read about in the *Daily News* years ago. Affectionately know as The Big House. The movie business had begun in New York at the beginning of the century, but D. W. Griffith and his merry nickelodeons had fled to California to escape the Edison patents, which threatened to lock up moviemaking. In The Big House the pioneer moviemakers, just about all dead now, had shot comedies and romances and cops-and-robbers starring the likes of Mary Pickford and Buster Keaton and Pearl White. Now it looked as though the studio served as a kind of resort hotel for the silver-screen idols of yesteryear. But many of them must've been dead too. If not all of them. And they looked the same as they had at the height of their movie careers. Maybe it was the ghosts of the idols I was seeing, but as far as I knew, I didn't believe in ghosts. Or maybe the atmosphere was being used as a screen and I was seeing reproductions of their images. In this high-tech age, anything seemed possible.

"Iggy! You're going to get us wiped out!" Marilyn screeched at me from the far end of the studio, her voice uncoiling eerily through the vast, musty, skylighted cavern. I flapped in her direction—not afraid of Syd and company so much as the unseen presences I felt swirling around in that theater of moldy dreams.

Marilyn's shout brought them out. Four or five men holding hammers and saws emerged from the storage and dressing rooms on both sides of the studio. I began to run, quickly catching up to Marilyn, who was shaking her ass too, heading for the exit on the far end. The carpenters began to run after us.

Down a curved staircase we fled, pounding and clanking with every leap on the metal steps. It seemed we were heading into the depths of hell, and in a few minutes I realized it was true. Through an heavy iron-clad door we pushed, and we stood inside a dim, damp cavern. All about us was the fiendish hardware of torture—the ribcrushers and swinging pendulum and back benders and bed of spikes and body stretcher. Before we could pivot and get the hell out of there, we were surrounded by Bella Lugosi and a band of his devils. Lugosi's eyes glowed like green coals, and though he wasn't smiling, somehow you knew he was happy to acquire a couple of victims.

"Come rrrrright in," said the Translyvanian, bowing slightly and sweeping his black cape open.

Marilyn and I were grabbed by the stony hands of his hairy-chested henchmen and yanked toward a steel chamber in the center of the cavern. One of the masked devils unbolted the riveted door and the others shoved the two of us inside. The iron rail bed and broken sink reminded me of a jail cell out of the movie *San Quentin.*

"*Now* what!" Marilyn said, as if annoyed over being delayed for a party.

Her question was answered soon enough. In a minute the temperature dropped fifty or sixty degrees, and I felt as if ice water had been pumped into the marrow of my bones. I was shaking so hard I could barely speak.

"What's the matter?" said Marilyn, who obviously didn't notice the change.

"I'm . . .free . . .zing."

"Must be catching a cold."

Soon I was trembling so wildly I fell over onto the bed, and Marilyn rushed over to me and cried out, "Are you okay, Iggy? What is it?" She actually sounded worried.

"My blood's . . .turning . . .to ice."

Through a speaker we heard the muffled voice of Lugosi. "Well, Mr. Lopes, are you ready to tell us wherrrrre you haf hid-dent the film?"

Marilyn looked up at the speaker and shouted, "He'll never tell you where it is!"

I had the awful feeling Lugosi was glad that Marilyn was being defiant, because the temperature dropped again, and I think I would've turned into a block of ice if the door hadn't swung open. By now I could barely see, but I heard a gruff voice say, "See, I told you you turned it down too much. People are frail—even a little chill can do them in."

The warmth surrounded me so quickly I was afraid my bones would crack, but in a few minutes I began to thaw and realized I would be okay. Only, I felt like a dishrag that had been kept in service too long. As my vision cleared, I saw all around us a gathering of the characters of cinema, grinning like gargoyles, the ones whose names you never knew but whose faces were familiar to you. Some of them were carrying torches, some gripped swords, one had a whip coiled in his large brown hands.

Now they got me up on my feet and forced us out of the chamber and down a long, wet, shadowy tunnel: something like the caves in *Journey to the Center of the Earth*. My feet seemed to be sticking slightly to the floor as we marched. Behind us the dark figures moved with stiff arms and legs, and every so often one of them would give us a shove.

"Keep your filthy hands off me!" Marilyn snapped at them.

Soon a light appeared, splashing out of a kind of amphitheater that was cut into rock. At one end of the arena was a great pit of fire spitting sparks. Jezuz! They were going to use me as a human sacrifice. As they pushed us forward, the mob began chanting—"Ooo-zom-bah, ooo-zom-bah." The heat was as intense as a steamed towel on the face. In the bright light from the long flames leaping out of the pit I could see that their eyes were irisless and their hairless scalps were oily. They were zombies.

On a low platform before the pit stood a man in a full-length, purple, hooded robe, and as we got close I recognized the cynical smirk of Claude Rains. Now he turned to face the flames, and raised both arms as if making an appeal to the devil. Suddenly Marilyn broke away from the zombies, rushed forward onto the platform, and shoved him from behind with both hands. Rains screamed maniacally as he disappeared from sight into the pit of coals. A puff of smoke flew up out of the pit, and there was a smell of burnt celluloid. The mob shrieked and was stunned into stillness, staring at the smoke. Marilyn grabbed my sleeve and pulled me around the pit and down a slimy passageway.

The zombies started after us, waving torches and swords and crying, "Ooo-zom-bah!"

The two of us ran as hard as we could, but the zombies kept gaining on us. At the end of the passageway was a long set of stairs, and I was certain that any energy I had left would be used up in the climb. Finally, we reached a metal door at the top and plowed through.

Suddenly, we were standing out under God's blue ceiling, on real grass. The kind they used to play baseball on. Marilyn pointed to the long white garage to the right, and I forced my aching legs to jog toward the side door. I could hear our fan club rushing out the basement trapdoor, shouting. Exhausted, I tripped and fell. I just couldn't go on. Marilyn disappeared inside. The zombies came at me, slicing their swords through the air. "Kill! Kill! Kill!"

I managed to get to my feet just as a classic cream-colored

convertible Chrysler came smashing through the front bay door. Glass and wood went flying, barely missing me. I had just enough oomph left to spring onto the running board of the rolling coupe, and finally to fall over the low door and onto the seat beside her. Marilyn slammed the iron stick into second and jammed the pedal to the floor. Behind us the gravel sparked into the dead eyes following us. Even as we widened the gap between us and them, the zombies kept running mindlessly, as if they were operated by batteries.

The folded-down canvas top flapped like Lugosi's cape as we peeled along the driveway, the tires outspinning the available friction—bits and pieces of the garage sailed off the grille and hood. On the slope rimmed by pines and birches I saw a scattering of the movie has-beens. Many of them stood up and watched us with a surprise that was noticeable even at that distance. Then they dropped their scrapbooks and started running in our direction. Guess they couldn't resist a good chase.

Someone must've called down ahead. As we roared between the ornamentals toward the entrance, the guards were hurrying to close the gates—having just opened them for Syd and Eric. They were too late. We swerved around the Packard. The guards sprang out of our way like jumping beans, and the Chrysler bulled open the gates. A quick inventory: one headlight lost, plus a fender curled like dried orange peel.

This Monroe had guts. Or else she was plain whacko. I braced my Hush-Puppies against the dashboard and fired off a prayer. "Please get me out of this goddamn mess!"

Marilyn didn't let up on the pedal, and as we bounded onto the county-maintained tar and slid right, I couldn't help but think she was going through a hell of a lot of trouble for someone I figured was working for the other side. I gazed at her until all that platinum hair and incandescent skin burned away my fear of being nailed to the cross.

$\bigtriangledown$

7
CHASE SEQUENCE

GOD'S BIG BRIGHT LENS was playing peek-a-boo behind a slab of clouds as the Chrysler roared down the road, straddling the white line.

"Hang on to your toupee!" Marilyn cried. "I'm headin' into this curve too. . . ." *Screeeeeech!*

In a complete circle we spun, and one breath before I blanked out, I thought: How does she know about my hairpiece? Most of my hair is real; the "toup" is only temporary. While I was covering a fire in a Harlem tenement for the *Squealer* my scalp got scorched by a flying windowsill. When I came out of my faint we were pouring straight ahead again, toward a crossroad being repaved by the county.

"I think we lost 'em!"

"Oooooh!" She sighed, as if I'd slipped my hand up her skirt.

A steamroller and dump truck and a tar vat, along with a small work gang, narrowed the road. Meanwhile, a gasoline tanker was barreling from the opposite direction toward the same keyhole as the Chrysler. The way I computed our distances and our respective speeds, the two vehicles figured to meet at the tightest juncture. Nevertheless, both vehicles rushed forward: we were being chased by thugs, and the truck was being wheeled by one of those hardheads who never gives an inch in an argument or on the road.

"We're not going to fit!"

"What'd you say?" she sirened into the gush of air.

Again I searched for the Director in the clouds, but He still wasn't ready to step in and block out his shots.

The wind took Marilyn's little white hat for a ride, and she swiveled her head back to look for it. "Doggone it!"

"Watch out!" I shouted. The gasoline truck couldn't have been more than twenty feet from our bumper when I yanked the wheel. The Chrysler sprang off the road like an albino panther, blasting a road horse into kindling and flattening a pyramid of sand and launching half a dozen members of the working class into a series of acrobatics. Scraping a huge old oak, we rumbled up a vast green turf—more like a golf course than a lawn—before stalling out.

I sat still, gasping.

"That hat was cute," Marilyn pouted, as if she'd known all along the script called for us to make it through okay.

Too shook up to say a word, I watched her sweep the hair off her nose, regain control of the wheel, crank up the engine, and swing down the slope toward the dirt walk.

The Chrysler chucked up some divots before whizzing onto the sticky road again. The inch-deep tracks we left in their soft black workmanship didn't make the road gang too happy. They raised their fists and started running in our direction. Everyone in the world seemed to be chasing us.

"Close call," Marilyn said cheerfully, nailing the pedal to the floor.

"There's two cars on our tail!" I realized out loud.

Even if it did tend to prove my theory about trouble coming in pairs, I wish I hadn't mentioned it. Marilyn Monroe already had problems controlling the hot developing fluid that ran in her veins. The sex symbol slammed the gear lever down dirty, and the coupe jolted forward. Once the old bomb built up some momentum, it could really roll, and we began putting space between us and them.

Split-level houses began to pop up on the streets as sudden as slices from a toaster. Marilyn, bearing down on the steering wheel, said: "If we can make it to the Expressway with a good lead, we'll leave 'em in the dust."

"At least we've lost the posse that was on foot."
Soon the houses were clustering in regular patterns, their lawns and shrubs sweeping past us. My fingers were notched into the heating vent for stability as we rumbled up a runway onto the Long Island Expressway. I wondered if the rest of the world knew about the silent-film factory of forgotten movie idols. It would make a good profile for the *Squealer*. But I probably didn't have a job anymore. Maybe the *News* would go for it; maybe a story like that would turn out to be a big break for me. Somehow I had to snap the spell that had gripped my life; I had to crawl out of that hole in the wall on Second Avenue, get back into the world, and begin to live again.

As we peaked the slope, Marilyn twirled us into the passing lane. A mile behind us I saw the twin trail of exhaust—two cruisers eating up the road. "They're gaining on us!"

"My hands!" she cried, staring at her grip on the wheel. "The skin on my hands is all cracked. All that damn heat down in the caverns!" She began to cry, the wind drying the tears almost as quickly as they swelled onto her cheeks.

Marilyn slid a silver flask out from under her seat. Unable to refuse her anything, I unscrewed it for her. But I couldn't help wondering how she'd known it was there. With one hand on the wheel, and the other elbow aimed at the sky, she took a belt.

"Don't you know it's against the law to drink while driving?"

"Why drive when we can fly!" she said gaily.

"'Cause I'd like to stick around long enough to cash at least one social security check."

She aimed her pink eyeballs at me and took another suck on the flask. Wising up, I wrenched the flask out of her fingers and took a slug too. Kicked in the skull by a mule wearing baseball spikes is how it hit me. "That stuff has enough octane to power a Mack truck."

"Bathtub gin."

"Least they could've done was strain the rings out of it."

The Chrysler coupe had less fenderware to haul than those sedans behind us, which meant that in a clear, straight run we could probably pull away from them. Our troubles weren't only behind us, though. We had to swerve around the Nissans and Plymouths and Chevys that were becoming too plentiful for the actuaries at Equitable Life. Meanwhile, the speedometer needle had jitterbugged past eighty and the car was shaking like it might fall to pieces.

"Let's not get too damn enthusiastic!"

Either she didn't hear me or didn't care. I spent the next few moments begging the Director to intervene—to get the fuzz to flag us down before we got into a game of leapfrog with a tractor-trailer. Chalk up another cliché as on the mark: You can never find the law when you really need it. But just try to spit on a subway platform at three in the morning. . . .

It was when Huntington (a remote huddle of shingled surfaces shimmering in the eastern haze) seemed to float past us that Marilyn bumped the back of a block-long golden

Caddy. As we swung around and pulled up alongside it, the guy at the wheel shook his fist at us.

"Your mother wears long johns," cried my pilot, waving V for victory.

It was only after the Caddy was eating our exhaust that I realized it was being driven by a cruel-mouthed Lionel Barrymore: Anyone who had played the roles of Ebenezer Scrooge *and* Old Man Potter had to look that way.

As we approached the edge of Queens, the traffic began to get sluggish. The Chrysler tiptoed along at fifteen or twenty miles per hour. Before our pursuers got tangled in the jam too, they were able to pull up to within a block or so behind us. But with all the moving cars between us, we were safe from them—at least for a while. This gave me time to ask a few questions.

"El Syd claimed the film is just a cultural curiosity, and yet he's willing to torture and kill for it. What's really going on?"

Marilyn unreeled those curly lashes in my direction. "Sydney starred in *Escape to Monte Carlo.*"

"You mean his ego's as fat as his ass and he doesn't want anyone to miss any of his films."

She glanced at me fiercely. Either one's ego or one's weight was a very touchy subject in Hollywood. "Sydney's been fading from the public's mind for years," she said. "Except for a small group of true fans who seek out old films, most people are not seeing Sydney's or Linda's or Lon's work anymore in theaters. And only rarely on late-night TV, when there's not much of an audience." She paused as if delivering memorized lines. "The only way any of us can carry on is through our films. But none of Syd's gang are superstars, so they stand to lose their place in the public's mind much faster. And in a much more final way."

More gibberish, I thought, and I took another swallow of mule juice, hoping it would kick some comprehension into me. "What good would getting hold of *Monte Carlo* do them?"

"Sydney believes if his lost film debuted in an important way in today's market it would kick up plenty of interest in him and his other films. He claims a major comeback could be launched and that his costars would be carried along on his coattails."

Syd had big enough coattails to carry an entire film studio along for a ride. But I didn't buy the rest of it.

Reading the skepticism in my face, Marilyn said with a faint shriek, "Don't you understand? They're afraid of being forgotten. Most of the others at The Big House have given up hope of ever regaining their standing with the public. All they do is live on the past through their scrapbooks, and by watching their movies over and over. It's pathetic. It's like they never performed, never existed."

"Sure I understand their not wanting to be forgotten. All of us have a problem with that idea," I said, checking over my shoulder to make sure they weren't creeping up on us. "What I can't figure is why Syd imagines a huge revival could be set off by one lousy film. It'll just end up on TV after midnight with the rest of the old flicks."

"Syd's got much bigger plans. For the past year, *Variety* has been reporting on the hottest combination network and syndication package ever assembled for television. ADC-TV and Vianet are calling it 'Black and White: A Dozen Diamonds of the Silver Screen.' "

"Sounds like another bunch of reruns."

"No, no," she insisted, glancing into the rearview mirror, though I couldn't be sure if she was looking for them or for her own face. "Before each film is shown they're going to have a top international critic discuss the work, and afterward they'll interview stars and character actors from the film. They've also come up with pieces of the films—the outtakes—that were never shown before. And sound and visual enhancements are being made. All of this is being tied up into a package they're billing as the finest dozen black-and-white films ever shot in America. And it's all backed up by a monster promotion budget."

"What films are they going to do?"

"Oh, things like *Sunset Boulevard* and *Citizen Kane* and *It's a Wonderful Life*."

"Not a bad concept," I admitted. "I'll probably tune in myself if I can ever get out of this mess."

"The project involves many millions of dollars, and if the syndicators reach their saturation goals there'll be thousands of airings in nearly five hundred markets in the U.S. and in something like a hundred and fifty countries around the world. Each of the twelve films in the lineup will rack up an enormous viewership."

"You don't mean to say Syd's entertaining the idea of getting *Escape to Monte Carlo* included in the package?"

"You bet."

"Haven't they already picked the dirty dozen?"

"Vianet cooked up an elaborate voting procedure, with critics from around the world casting ballots, and each month they release the name of another film to be included. It's all hype that let's them play it safe in case market sales are not up to expectations. As of now, not all of the films have been named. And Syd's gambling that if he could get international attention in the press for a film never seen by the public, the syndicators might slip *Monte Carlo* into the schedule to boost sales."

"With a title like that and all those hams in it, frankly, I have serious doubts *Monte Carlo* would qualify as a fine film, much less one of the best ever."

"You're a sweetheart, Iggy, but you're also naive. It's all money. In the past month or so, sales of the package have dropped off, and with Vianet out on a limb with a big promotion outlay by the network, they could well go for it. Showing *Monte Carlo* would amount to a world premiere forty years after the fact. Besides, Joe Mankiewicz directed, and that man never made anything but quality films." Seemed to me it was Mankiewicz who'd directed her in a bit role in *All About Eve*.

Suddenly I noticed that many of the cars around us had pulled away from our vehicle, and the drivers kept glancing from the road in front of them to our car. It occurred to me then that I'd been cruising along in a collector's Chrysler having a conversation with a dead actress, and I wondered whether the other motorists recognized her—or could they see her at all? If not, why was *I* able to see her? Had I croaked without knowing it, or did I have some special power? These questions had to be put on hold, however, because the opening made by the cars trying to get out of our way had enabled Greenstreet and Chaney, chauffeured by Von Stroheim, to move up within gunsight distance.

Syd raised his hand up to the open window.

"Look out!" I yelped. "He's got a gun."

Just as I tasted the rubber floor mat a hollow pop sounded, as if a cap gun had gone off. But Marilyn still sat straight up in her seat, wheeling the car. Now the traffic brought the Chrysler to a toupee-loosening halt, and peeking over the rim of the door I spotted Wolfman making his way toward us on foot. His right paw was buried in the pocket of his jacket.

"Chaney's closing in."

"Come on," Marilyn ordered, opening the door and hopping out, her glands jumping beneath her dress. I hit the pavement too, keeping low and right on her tail. Naturally, the traffic picked that time to start up again. The drivers bashed their horns as we dodged around the vibrating fenders.

Hoisting herself up the back loading step of a truck, Marilyn tumbled behind the flap of canvas. I did the same—a happy landing right on top of her. Lord, she is soft! It turned out to be a laundry truck with a couple of tons of Long Island's soiled shirts and socks aboard. I stuck my nose out the canvas to see if we'd been spotted. The Studebaker was about half a block behind us, trying to weasel past other vehicles, its horn blasting steadily, and the boss's car was jerking impatiently along beside it. Chaney stood on his toes on the running board of the stalled Chrysler coupe, checking out the other vehicles.

I sank down onto a laundry sack. "I don't think they saw us climb in here."

"Aaaah!" she said, rubbing the insides of her thighs with satisfaction.

I got an erection, or maybe it was the same one that had woken me that morning.

Miss MM and I shared a grin over our temporary security. With her I would've shared anything, even a grave. But my smile was as fake as Geppetto's son. Behind it was this barbarous headache: partly from the tension of the high-speed chase; partly that ceaseless erection; and partly because there were so many unanswered questions still cluttering my brain.

All of the silver in my teeth I would've traded for a white tablet, any white tablet. "You don't happen to have an aspirin on you?"

With stiff lips she said: "Sorry, honey. I used my last one."

The head balanced tenuously on my shoulders throbbed

thunderously as I remembered exactly how poor Norma Jean had used it.

Sprawled on a flattened laundry bag, sipping from the flask, Marilyn said, "You're wondering why I'm sitting in a truck with you instead of riding in the Packard with them."

I don't trust people—even dead people—who read minds, so I kept my mouth shut.

"Sex queens stick in the mind a lot longer than fat cats and horror freaks, so people are still watching my movies and talking about me and hanging up my posters. Sometimes there's even a book by some creep I bedded down with once or twice. And the reporters still can't get me out of their dirty minds. I don't always like what they write, but as they say in show biz, as long as they spell your name right."

I would have defended my fellow reporters if it weren't true: we often bend the truth to make a story out of dust. It was also true that the previous resident of my room had left Marilyn's famous nude poster—her white skin sprawled over red satin—tacked to the ceiling of my john. But it still didn't jive. "Why do you want the film?"

"Syd's desperate to protect his immediate future," she said, eyeing me. "What I want is to promote my long-distance future, and that's going to take money."

Maybe Marilyn and I had more in common than I'd realized, with both of us after money and both on the run from Syd. "You're lucky they didn't rub you out at The Big House."

She laughed. "To do that, they'd have to get hold of every copy of every film I ever made and destroy them all."

The more I learned, the less I knew. "Why did it all hit the fan now?"

"Sydney's got a scheme to show the film at the Academy Awards. If he could pull it off, there'd be just the level of international media coverage he'd need to force the syndicators to include it in the 'Black and White' package."

"When are the Awards, anyway?"

Marilyn looked at me oddly, as if I couldn't remember my own birthday. "April first."

I checked my calendar watch. "That's today!"

To the back of the truck I went to review thug and traffic conditions. Pushing the canvas aside, I found myself face-to-face with a roly-poly man who looked remarkably like Alfred Hitchcock, and who seemed just as surprised to be pulling himself up the back of the truck as I was to find him there. My fist sank into his neck. The feeling and sound were not quite the softness and slap of human flesh. He peeled off the back end of the two-ton like cellophane off a Twinkie, splashing onto the long black hood right behind us. I hated to do it to old Hitch—a favorite of mine—but everyone's got a right to protect himself.

All three cars—the Packard, the Studebaker, the Chrysler—had caught up to us. And though it wasn't easy to say for sure, I could've sworn the Studebaker was being driven by the good Mr. Belvedere—Clifton Webb, with that animated mustache of his.

El Syd poked his rod out the side window, and I bellyflopped into the sacks. Two burn spots appeared in the canvas.

Miss MM drew her eyes away from the cracked skin of her hands and said casually, "Too bad you had to dump Alfred—he's a good film man. But he asked for it."

"They've got us surrounded, Marilyn! Help me with these sacks."

Marilyn looked slightly confused, but she got up. A lot of Long Islanders would go to work with rings around their collars next week, I thought as I hooked the end of the canvas flap up to the top of the truck and started rolling one bag after another out the back. Marilyn got the idea and helped. "What fun!" she chimed. The sacks thudded against the cars. Suddenly a screech and *kaplam! kaplam! kaplow!*

"Bull's-eye!" Marilyn chirped.

The Packard had stopped short, setting off a chain reaction of crashes involving another half a dozen cars. The Chrysler had brushed off the Studebaker, which veered away and red-dogged a bridge abutment. *Kerplash!* The Stude's engine flashed, and instantly the entire car was wrapped in flames. . . . I cried out, "Mr. Belvedere! Mr. Hitchcock!"

Marilyn seemed amused.

$\triangledown$

8

MANSION CAPER

WHEN THE TRUCK PULLED up for a red light, Marilyn slid out the back onto the tar. I did the same. Our descent from the general direction of heaven startled a rich trick in tweed who was steering a pair of French poodles to the curb, one powder blue, one sky pink: even purebreds have to pee. It felt good to be back on the island of bedrock, the city that never sleeps, and like a homing pigeon I had Second Avenue on the brain. But Marilyn took my arm and pumped her legs west down Seventy-sixth Street, pulling me along.

Though I wanted to go home—if a dump like that deserves such a fine name, I let her lead me on. Maybe I just wanted to be seen with a bombshell. Maybe I was curious about how my fellow Manhattanites were going to react to seeing Monroe back on the streets. But no one even glanced our way, and it was hard to tell if it was because they couldn't see her or because Manhattanites are too self-involved to notice even a dead movie star strutting along their streets. Once again I wondered about the condition of my life, or existence, or whatever it was I was carrying around on my back from day to day. I sulked as we headed toward Fifth Avenue, bobbing past the smooth stone facades of Money Row.

While the rest of the Big Apple was caught up in a continual cycle of breaking down the old and building up the new, this stretch of artsy-fartsy shops and high-society residences *never* changed. Ovals of thick plate glass glimmered down at us like huge monocles. Brass doorknobs gleamed shamelessly through ten thousand coats of polish, rubbed by hired hands. The steps were hardened gingerbread, impaled by chrome-dipped handrails . . . to support the begrudging, twig-legged dowagers creeping up and down, both feet settling on every step, for the space of two lifetimes each. The rich had learned how to squeeze double mileage out of that ancient roué, Time.

"One of these days," I promised out loud, gazing at the brownstone castles that guarded the street. "One of these days."

Marilyn glanced at me as if I weren't making any sense. Now that she had made it to the top, she didn't want to remember how, as a frail, perfect, illegitimate butterfly, she had fluttered with all her innocence after a star—and seized it. Or rather, was seized by it. That fact of her life put us as far apart as Monte Carlo was from the South Bronx. And with the world divided into stars and star-gazers, eventually Marilyn had to give me the shaft. It went with her station. So why not get the jump on her?

"See you around, sugar," I said, strutting through the veil of gray bus exhaust.

Behind me I heard the *snick-snick-snick* of spiked heels on concrete. "Angel," she breathed, "why are you running out on me?"

Don't stop, legs! But they didn't listen, dragging to a halt as a soft white hand cupped my sagging shoulder. Even with cracked skin, it was a sexy hand.

"Sweetie," she chirped, her blue eyes rippling like that pond the Fresh Air Fund had sent me to upstate as a kid, "listen to me just a sec. And if you still feel the same, I won't try to sway you."

A sucker for any blonde with a sob story, I said, "Make it snappy."

She toed real close, so I could *feel* her words on my forehead. "One block away there's a film worth enough to put you and me on top of the world for the rest of eternity. We could set up house in Beverly Hills *and* Palm Beach *and* Park Avenue *and* Monte Carlo."

Even if her values—like mine—stunk all the way to the Stock Exchange, she still smelled like daisies to me.

"With a swimming pool?" I said weakly.

"And a riding stable."

"And a miniature golf course?"

Marilyn eyed me exotically. While I had a taste for bucks, I had no idea whether that film was stashed at Goldwine's or not, and when actually faced with a choice between freedom and cash, I had to pause and do a heavy think on which of the two was more necessary to my well-being. At first the Dow Jones on being footloose went sky high. On the other hand, I'd floated around long enough to know money could be cashed into freedom. If you had a big bankroll no one dared turn his back on you, whether you needed a heart transplant or ringside seats at the Garden.

"Iggy,"—she said, sighing, "there's a lot of big cushy beds at Stan Goldwine's. Why don't we go and try out a few of them?"

Marilyn plucked a brass key from her bra, inserted it into a notch in the iron door, twisted, and we were inside. If she just happened to have a key tucked in her titty, something had to be rotten in Paradise.

Irrationally I followed her . . . into a reception area that seemed to have been lifted whole out of Grand Central

Station: gouged stone pillars, tiled walls, scuffed marble floors. Tailed and horned gargoyles of stone sat watching us from a ledge where the ceiling met the walls. Except for the paintings that had been removed—the rims of dust on the walls were testimony—everything seemed to be the same as it was the night Goldwine was blown apart. Right down to the brass umbrella stand the size of a trash can, and what still looked to me like a motorcycle rack. The place was so huge the butler had to scoot around on a Harley, I guess. Deeper in the hall stood an onyx ashtray stand in the shape of a naked lady. Nice figure. Far off several pieces of furniture were hunched under sheets. The thousand-year-old carpet seemed weeks away from melding with the mansion's ritzy decay. On its fading tulip pattern stood one courtly, claw-footed, high-backed chair, not covered, as if awaiting the return of Goldwine himself. I guess he was rich enough to buy his way back from the dead.

For all the money this fat cat had piled up—more than twenty million, according to *Newsweek*—he had lived kind of moldily, like a great civilization in decline. No surprise. In my wanderings for the *Squealer* I'd learned that middle-class folks often lived more plush than the wealthy. People with dough wake up each morning with the terror of finding themselves broke. Poor things had to be careful with every penny.

Kicking up the dust as we moved down the corridor, I slipped my arm behind Marilyn and set my hand into the notch of her waist.

"Once we have the film"—she smiled that smile—"you'll get all you can handle."

"Promises, promises."

"Don't worry your pretty head." She laughed strangely. "It's what I was built for. I'm the sweet angel of sex."

I'd read that description of her somewhere years ago, but her tone was sardonic.

"Which way?"

"Uh . . . follow me."

Something, call it reporter's instinct, told me it was true: that the film actually was stashed in the mansion, if it was anywhere at all. And one way I might get to dive into the sack with the sweet angel of sex was to turn private eye and locate the film. It was the one thing that seemed to get her hot. Besides, if I leveled with her—told her I really didn't know where it was—she wouldn't believe me.

"Where do you have it hidden?"

"Give me a minute to get reoriented."

I stopped, turned, looked behind us.

"Well?" she said.

"Not so fast, not so fast," I said like Frank Morgan under pressure to produce a little wizardry in the Land of Oz. "I've only been in this railroad terminal once in my life for a couple of minutes."

She looked at me sort of funny, but kept her heart-shaped lips zippered.

I stood dead center in the hall, a studious dent across my forehead, checking the routes open to me—up the nearby staircase, into one of four doors that led off the roundup area, or down a flight at the far end. Since the beds figured to be overhead, I spun around and pointed. "Up those stairs."

Gripping the oak banister, I moved up slowly, Marilyn tailing me. I was going to have to come up with something quick, a prospect that, while worrisome in certain respects, was pleasing in another. Playing detective was romantic stuff to me. It suited my personality. I was forever sniffing out the lives of strangers at bars, or hapless characters like Ferdy and Monica at the office, wondering how their love lives had hit the rocks, how they got started in crime. Now all those paperbacks I'd read and movies I'd seen could be put to some practical use. Yeah, I thought, I'll style myself after Mike Hammer: track down the film and, while I'm at it, nail Marilyn to the mattress and, to make it a grand slam, tackle Goldwine's killer. Get the girl, the money, *and* my picture in the *New York Post*.

On my previous sortie through Goldwine's New York stronghold the police arrived before I'd gotten above the first landing, so I didn't know what to expect upstairs. And since I had no particular place to look for the film, I figured I might as well locate a mattress and suggest a sex break.

Though it was late morning, there was barely enough light to see into a sort of drawing room that had dull, bare walls. And no beds. Just a bunch of chairs and a few tables under sheets, plus half a dozen stands to collect the ashes of the people who used to wait to see the big G. You've got to go through a lot of cigarettes to reach someone *that* powerful. Fact is, I could've used a smoke myself. I started biting my nails instead.

"Is it in here, or isn't it?"

Without a peep I skidded toward the doorknob across the hall. Marilyn stayed at my hip like a Siamese twin, a skeptical slit between her long black lashes. Twisting the knob and entering, I was disappointed once again: a partly sheeted, massive desk, three chairs also under wraps, backgrounded by a wall of shelves tight with books—real books—that they must've tried to boil down to scripts. There was a spade-shaped stain about the size of a tin film case on the unicorn on the rug, and I wondered if Judy Garland had spilled a glass of Four Roses when she was looking to make a comeback deal. Maybe Randolph Scott had spit into the brass cuspidor in the corner. The mossy green drapery stunk of ancient cigar smoke, crystalized perfume, evaporated tears.

While it wasn't a boudoir, there was a bit of a sofa that could've supported a pair of beings, assuming they were short, assuming they went double-decker. "Why don't we rest our bones," I said, eyeing the brown velvet arm that stuck out from the white coverlet.

"For goodness' sake, Iggy. Any minute Syd's boys'll be kicking our heads off our shoulders."

Obviously she had lured me into the mansion without any intention of creaking the mattress springs. There was no sense in losing my head over her: I decided to get out of that haunted house.

"Marilyn, I'm gonna give it to you straight."

"I sure wish you would—and fast."

Just then there was a loud crash downstairs, like someone had made an emergency entrance through a window.

"Get out of sight and stay put," she said with a managerial grasp of the situation. "I'll see what's happening."

A second before she turned to move toward the stairs she lifted the hem of her silky dress and drew a compact, chrome automatic out of a holster strapped to her gam. It was a pretty piece of jewelry, even though it was designed to punch .32-caliber holes in human beings.

My legs churned down the hall, intent on catching an express out of there. I cut into another corridor, just as long, and made my way through the interior dimness, past matching, puffy-assed chairs, a low table bearing a quarter inch of dust, and a long glass case that had been emptied of its trophies—a parade of Oscars? At the end stood a human-size statue shrouded by a blanket. It gave me the creeps.

Below there were faint voices, the crunching of glass under foot. Up the stairs I went, two at a time. The staircase opened into a broad hall with ten or twelve rows of padded theater chairs facing a hundred square feet of white screen in the wall. A glass-enclosed popcorn machine stood robotlike in the corner. Wow! They didn't even have to leave the joint to go to the movies. All-time blockbusters must've been reeled for the first time in this private theater, with dozens of top stars in attendance and a wild party following each screening. For a moment my mind could see James Mason forcing Sue Lyon to sit on his lap as she sucked on a cherry, heart-shaped lollipop.

A door at the back of the theater! I made my way to it down the aisle between the seats, past the projection booth. Opening the door, feeling up the wall, I found the light switch. On the high ceiling three bare bulbs blinked on. No exit, and no place to hide. Just a cramped, oblong storage room with thousands of film tins lined up in steel racks, floor to ceiling. As I backed out, there was a brittle, muffled crack of a pistol downstairs.

"Marilyn!"

The voices grew louder, and I was wishing I had a stunt man to step in for me. But you have to be a star before they hire some fool to risk his neck in your name. As usual, though, fate took care of the arrangements. I tripped over the leg of a chair and flew full weight into a panel of wall which, upon contact with my head, swung wide open. As I fell into a heap inside, I heard them pounding up the stairs. The panel swung closed.

9

BOOBY PRIZE

THE HARD-HITTING VOCAL CHORDS were shockingly familiar: "Doesn't look like anyone was wid her."

"Been claiming all along she wants nothing to do with the film," said a familiar female voice, "and yet we find her here. You figure it out."

"She wasn't fooling me a second."

"Cut the yappin' and keep checkin'."

"Yeaah, yeaah, yeaah."

"How's about you, Joanie? Onto anything?"

"Hard to see the titles in this chintsy light. Why don't we run them on a moviola?"

"You nuts? It'll take too long. Use one of the flashlights."

"What if Goldwine had the leader for a different feature spliced onto it?"

That bright idea knocked them silent.

Movie history told me there had to be a way to see out of the secret compartment into the theater. It just took a while to find it. My finger touched a disk on the panel in front of me. Carefully I put my eye to the peephole, confirming what my ears had been telling me. I was eavesdropping on a give-and-take between Gable, Crawford, and Robinson. Each was

costumed the way they had been for one of their big movies;
skinny Joan in a heel-length, form-fitting ice-blue gown;
plug-shaped Edward G. in a double-breasted, pin-striped
suit; and straight-shouldered Clark with his fedora shoved
back and white shirt-sleeves rolled up. . . . Dead, I said to
myself, every last one of them *dead*. What the hell was
happening to the world? Why couldn't they keep dead people
dead and living people alive?

When I shifted my legs to get the blood flowing in my feet
again, something fell with a dull clank behind me. I gave up
breathing as all three out in the theater stopped, glanced at
one another. Ever so gently I lowered the peephole disc,
leaving the barest crack. Gable took two steps in my direction, his face compressed with suspicion. He listened hard
for a long while, looked at the others again, and said, "Just
a rat in the woodwork."

Phew!

I'd gotten a fairly good look at Gable's mug, and couldn't
help wondering what all the fuss was about. Even *my* ears
looked less like cauliflower. And my skin wasn't so bumpy,
either. Only in the chin department—his was sharp as a
cinder block—did he have something over me. Mine is
pointy without making any particular point.

Clark swaggered to the door, stuck his neck out, and
rumbled, "Hey, you guys! Put Marilyn on ice and come on
up here. We need your help to check out these damn films."

After several minutes, into the room straggled Spencer
Tracy and John Wayne, each with his unforgettable drag,
those trademarks that were stamped into the minds of
America. Wayne was wearing a Stetson and western jeans
and tooled boots, and Tracy wore a short-sleeve white shirt
and a pair of gray sharkskin trousers. Bright pennies gleamed
in the slots of his loafers.

"You take care of Marilyn?"

"In dreamland," piped Tracy.

Clark pointed them to the film-storage room, and when Wayne spied the film racks he sputtered, "Holy Jehozaphat! There's enough of them, ain't there?"

"Why d'ya think I made the bunch of you come along?" Tracy shook his head at the rows of film.

"Don't just stand there!" Gable barked.

Wayne and Tracy marched into the back room, and each came out with a batch of film tins. They sat down on theater seats and started opening them, holding the celluloid up to the fuzzy light. Edward G. looked angry as he stumped into the back room to get another stack. Gable and Crawford followed.

"Say! Here's *The Green Berets*!" piped Wayne. "One of my all-time favorites."

Tracy glanced at him with glassy eyes.

After several minutes of relative quiet, Crawford complained, "My nails are getting ruined!"

"Just keep openin' those tins," Clark grunted.

"We're wasting our time," grumbled Edward G. "The reporter's the key to this thing."

At the mention of me a chill shot up my spine, lodged at the base of my neck, and started throbbing like it might go off.

"Our man at The Big House said Syd worked him over and didn't get a thing," Tracy said.

"If you ask me," said Crawford, "it's sitting pretty in one of Goldwine's safes at his penthouse in L.A. They say he had half a dozen built into the joint."

"Me and Cooper went through that place from the cushions to the chandeliers," claimed Wayne. "It's clean, I tell ya, clean."

"Did you find all the safes?"

"Far as I know."

"Maybe we should've gotten hold of Orson and turned

him loose in this joint. He's so intense he might've come up with something."

"You kidding? He's so full of himself he's incapable of imagining even for a moment that his film would get bumped from the syndication deal to make way for Syd's."

"If only Jimmy Stewart were one of us, at least he'd bring a little calm thinking into this process."

"Or maybe Ray Milland."

"This is ridiculous—we're getting nowhere."

"Stop your griping, all a ya," said Gable. "You've all got a lot at stake in this thing. There are only twelve spots. Just remember that."

Just then Wayne glanced toward the far wall at a huge mirror—figures there'd be a huge mirror—and looked at himself a few moments, as if he wasn't entirely sure one of his films was included in the Vianet package. I couldn't think of any he'd done, except maybe *The Quiet Man*, that would be worthy of such a distinction. But that'd been in color. Maybe Gable had lied to him and said he knew that *Stage Coach* would be included. Or more likely Wayne's ego had gotten the best of him.

"Once the Awards are finished, Syd's finished anyway," said Joan.

"Maybe yes, maybe no."

"The syndication package goes on the air in a few months. There's no way they're gonna find another event as big as the Awards to grab the spotlight, and it's already getting too late even for that."

"I wouldn't be so sure about that," said Tracy. "It's three hours earlier on the coast, so they still have plenty of time to cause trouble at the Oscars."

"If we don't find the film here," said Gable, "there's a damn good chance Syd and his mob already got hold of it and we're gonna have to fly out to L.A."

In my mind I could see them flapping their arms like wings at 35,000 feet.

"There must be ten thousand films back there!" Edward G. complained.

"We'll be here 'til the Emmys," said John, completing the thought.

Clark stopped opening a film tin, looked at them, and said: "You mean to say you're willing to risk having your film dropped and losing the standing you've built up with the public out of sheer laziness? You people amaze me. I really mean it—you *amaze* me."

"Clark's right. Bad enough we've got to compete with all the new actors coming on the scene, but to compete with second-raters from the past is ridiculous."

"I just do not understand why somebody didn't go through these films a long time ago."

"Gary and I started the job way back," said Gable. "But we never finished. It was too much for two men. Hell, this is the first time I've been able to get any cooperation from you highfalutin *stars*."

"If it was here, I think Syd would've found it—he's always so thorough."

"Except for one thing. I've got a hunch the reporter doubled back after the place'd been searched and stashed it in one of these cans. Leaving it right under everybody's noses. Just like the Purloined Letter."

"I didn't know you read much, Clark," said Tracy, grinning as he opened another can.

"I saw the movie."

In the wringer of a war between two gangs I was caught: the superstars who wanted to keep their top billing, and the lesser lights of the screen who were losing their place on the memory lanes of the human mind. But Marilyn, as big a star as any of them, had been knocked out cold by the Gable team, and this didn't make sense to me.

"If more hotshots would climb down off their high horses and help out," said the Duke, prying open another can, "we'd be through these cans *tout suite*."

Tracy said, "Folks like Mr. Grant and Mr. Bogart think they're too exalted to soil their hands in a projection booth."

"And they'll be the first ones to bellyache when they get elbowed out of the box office," Edward said.

"I'm still shocked Bogart turned his back on us," piped Joan, holding another strip of film to the light.

"After all the time Humphrey worked with Syd, he could've been a *big* help," Gable admitted.

"Well, I can't fault him for that," drawled Wayne. "Turning against his old sidekick would've been like double-crossing his horse."

"You overgrown Boy Scout!" Crawford spitfired. "Clark and Spencer are right. The public's heart is a jungle. We're fighting for our survival. If they bump my film, I just won't be able to face eternity."

"What makes you so sure one of your films will be in the final package?"

"They wouldn't dare pass up *Mildred Pierce*—my fans would storm Vianet's headquarters!"

"Let's not get overly emotional," said Tracy with midwestern stoicism, "or we'll obscure our primary purpose, which is to inspect each and every one of these films."

Ten or fifteen minutes of opening and checking the film tins passed before Crawford said to Gable, "Even if we did find the film, what would we do with it?"

"What the hell do you think we're going to do with it, hold a film festival?" exploded Edward G. Robinson, throwing a film tin on the floor with a clatter, causing me to flinch. "We've got to destroy it, of course!"

"Or maybe we should lock it up in a safe place," said Spencer Tracy, "and let this deal blow over. Regardless of our feelings about it, *Escape to Monte Carlo* is important to cinematic history."

"Can the sentimentality!" piped Robinson.

"Probably just a dud anyway," said Wayne, prying open another film tin.

"That film is more than history," Gable interjected. "And it's more than a gun in our back. It's an opportunity."

Not sure what he was getting at, John Wayne tugged the rim of his Stetson. And I shifted my ass, which was falling asleep.

"All we've got to do is stash that film under a rock until those characters are only a footnote in a book about the movies. Then we dust it off and sell it to some private collector abroad as the last of its kind. No fuss, no fanfare. The public wouldn't even know about it. Finally we work out a deal with a promoter to turn that cash into T-shirts and posters and magazines with our faces plastered on 'em. That way we could bury Syd and his crew forever *and* boost our own standing with the public."

Crawford looked at Gable with a touch of the reverence his fans accorded him. But it was movie love, not the kind between a real man and a real woman.

"You romantic leads need some sense—some cold, hard facts—knocked into your heads," declared Edward G. "I'm not taking any chances. If I get my hands on that film, my lighter comes out and *Monte Carlo* goes up in smoke."

Gable glared at him.

Fame is power, and that's what they were really arguing over in the screening room. But now they all looked powerless.

Bewildered as to what they should do next, one by one they gave up the job of inspecting the film tins and filtered out of the theater. Silence and shadows swiftly filled their places. I stayed put, wondering what they had done with Marilyn, or if she had been decoying me and really *was* working with Gable. If so, then they would've known I was somewhere in the mansion. And if that was the deal, wouldn't she have turned that shiny automatic on me?

At last I felt safe enough to step out of the secret compartment, which is when I kicked the object that had fallen earlier. Reaching down in the dark, I picked up a flat, metal disc. My hands shook as I moved quietly but quickly through the films scattered on the floor to the storage room, switched on the light, and pried open the film tin with my fingernails. In a minute I verified what I'd feared and, at the same time, what I'd hoped: I was holding *Escape to Monte Carlo*, with the Abominable Boss getting top billing and The Wolfman right up there too. It also featured the slick, if sour-hearted, Linda Darnell. The rest of the names were too small to make out on celluloid.

With the missing film in my hands I had become instantly powerful, at least among those who wanted it so bad. But it also meant that as soon as I lost control of the film, I would become utterly expendable. Wasn't it just like fate to tie my fortune, my survival, to a piece of celluloid, a booby prize that could go off like a bomb at any moment?

"Why me?" I asked the light bulb just before cutting off its power supply.

The film tucked in the front of my trousers, my jacket buttoned, I tiptoed down the curved stairway, my eyes wide and strained and, probably, bloodshot—on the lookout for bodies living and dead. Apparently they had taken Marilyn with them. I had the place to myself. But I didn't want it.

Quickly through the main assembly area I went, ever so lightly over the seemingly endless runway of carpet, past the nudie ashtray, the high-backed chair—still empty—out the heavy door, and down the tier of granite steps.

Through the lumpy, liquid atmosphere I waded, along a Fifth Avenue thick with the slow-going cars and buses and delivery trucks of midday. Sucking in the mix of carbon monoxide and oxygen greedily, I cut east on foot.

$\triangledown$

10
OLD FLAME

I DIDN'T KNOW WHAT I needed more—some cold cash to emigrate to New Jersey, or a good piece of ass to keep me out of Creedmore loony bin. Either way, there was only one person I knew who had cash *and* ass to spare, and who might be willing to share a little of both with me: Judy Plane. Last summer I had spent one wild Saturday night in her apartment. Her two rooms were cramped, but that Castro convertible had plenty of spring! True, it was the only night we ever spent in bed together. Once you've gone to the well, though, it's hard to give up the idea that you can't drink there again, some time or other, under some circumstance or other.

I couldn't get the day of the week straight in my mind. But since Judy worked the night shift, I figured I could probably catch her at home—unless she was at the local bar and grill picking up something, or someone, for dinner. I started jogging toward East Eighty-eighth. By the time I reached her block the film had fallen out of my trousers only twice.

If Judy wasn't ready to climb back into the sack the moment I walked through her door—hell, it'd been a good eight months—maybe she would help me out with a loan.

She made good bucks as a computer programmer. And if she wasn't ready to float a few quid in my direction as soon as I finished my first cup of coffee, maybe I could convince her to let me hide out in her apartment with the film until I could figure out my next move.

Too bad it hadn't worked out between us. When we were scraping the crusts out of our eyes on the morning after, she'd taken one look at me and said, "Who the hell are you?" I took it personally and beat it, but later on I realized she'd been too groggy and hung over to know what she was saying, so I gave her a call. We talked a little while and she sounded kind of interested. I told her I'd take her out to dinner pretty soon, and I meant it. But I never called back, because I started thinking she was probably just leading me on. One of these days I had to stop being so damn sensitive. Today was as good a time as any to begin. Who knows? Maybe we could get it together. I might be coming into some money pretty soon, and what good is money without someone besides yourself to spend it on?

As I approached her building—an eight-story, staggered stack of celery-green bricks, I checked over my shoulder. Near as I could tell, I hadn't been tailed. I tucked myself into the outer hall. When I saw her name was still in a slot, I felt encouraged and pressed the button. Without asking who was there, Judy buzzed me inside. She shouldn't take chances like that. Never know who you might let in.

I pushed my body into the bare lobby: it had that peculiar smell that seems bred into the lobbies of New York but that is actually caused by years of overcooked foods and underwashed diapers, the essences of which are absorbed by the plaster walls and ceiling, the tile floor. The fireplace, painted the color of granite, was a fake. So were the blue posies in the cracked vase on the mantel. At that moment everything in the world seemed fake, and I'd already lost hold of my upbeat feeling.

I entered the elevator and was hoisted straight up. All the way I kept thinking about the cable that was lifting me off the surface of the earth, that my life hung from a single silver thread. Suppose that thread were weak at some point, frayed by the constant rubbing against circumstances. Any moment it could snap and that would be the end of me. No twenty-one-gun salute. No eulogy from the mayor for dying in the line of duty. Not even a loyal dog to howl beside my body. Just gone. By the time I docked at the sixth floor, I was shaking.

Cautiously I moved up to her door, standing slightly aside so she couldn't peek at me through the peephole. Suddenly afraid to face her, I stood there thinking over things. Judy Plane could hardly be classified as centerfold material—more like a wallflower with hidden passion. But she was friendly and as short as me, so I'd felt comfortable around her. After a few minutes with her, I'd lost the need to wisecrack my way through a conversation.

I often think about that night. I sat down on a stool beside her at the Hellzapoppin and she turned to me immediately and said, "Hi!"

I was so surprised I couldn't think of a reply at first, but I finally sputtered, "Do you come to this bar often?"

"Oh, no, this is the first time." She smiled. It was odd how you could never meet a woman in a bar who had ever been there before. But what could I expect, prowling a singles bar in the hope of finding true love? If Judy was a barfly, it was just because she was a victim of the same powerful loneliness that held me in its grip.

In ten minutes she'd had her hand on my knee, telling me the story of her life. It wasn't a sex signal so much as a need to make human contact, and I placed my hand on hers. In retrospect, her story wasn't that interesting, but that night, balanced on a swivel stool, the tale of her being born and going to the Grace Episcopal Church and falling in love with the boy next door and graduating from high school in Barnesville, Indiana, sounded fascinating. Four or five beers will do wonders for your powers of appreciation.

The buzzer cup centered by the button looked like a miniature brass breast, and I placed my thumb on the black nipple and pressed gently, so as not to disturb her too much. The door opened instantly, as if she'd been standing there waiting all those months for me to come back. There she was, five-foot-two, eyes of ocher, with the crooked front teeth and the flat chest but that certain *je ne sais quoi*.

For a moment we didn't move, looking at each other, solemn and unsure, and then she said, "Creep!" and slammed the door shut.

The word "creep" kept bouncing around the corners of my brain as I shuffled along the solitary street, and I cursed my mother and father for having brought me into so heartless and cruel a world. What did Judy mean, "Creep"? Why couldn't she have just said, "Get lost!" Or "Where the hell've you been?" Or "Drop dead!" Why did she have to say "Creep"?

After drifting a few blocks aimlessly, I got into a telephone booth and shut the door. I was lucky to find one—even phone booths were dying off, so you had to stand out in the noise and cold if you wanted to connect with someone. Before long they would figure a way to make all human contact impossible. I stood very still, like a man waiting for the chamber to fill up with gas, wondering who I could call, wondering what I would say. I thought about dialing Monica at the office, but she had called me a creep once too. Finally I dug my wallet out of my jacket and looked for the massage-parlor card on the back of which I had my mother's area code scribbled. Must've been months since I'd called. Her old man wasn't going to like getting a collect call from me, but this was an emergency.

It took years but my mother had managed to escape the Bronx, finally letting go of the fantasy that my father would come back from wherever it was he himself had escaped to. Dad dreamed of riding in Rolls-Royces, but all he did was drain the oil out of Chevys. Where Mom picked up his replacement I can't say—the Blarney Stone Bar, I suppose. But Bert something or other, an accountant out of the Newark branch of Lerner's, kept up the mortgage on their quarter acre in Teterboro and made her the beneficiary of a fifteen-percent discount on winter coats. A little security is all Mom had ever asked out of life, and she had achieved it, so I guess she was content. What did it matter that Bert had a face that belonged on a groundhog and a mind as dull as a dead battery?

The phone rang and rang. At last there was a clickety-click, and a cold, dry, recorded voice came on: " . . . numbah you have diahled has been disconnect . . ." Bert what's-his-name was too steady to miss paying enough phone bills to get his service cut off. That could only mean one thing—they had moved. How could my mother move without giving me word? What a world! Even mothers were running out on their offspring. Come to think of it, she had once called me a creep too. . . .

I started floating again in the general direction of my room. A city was out there around me, but I couldn't see the people gliding by too well, and I didn't smell the fumes, and the honking traffic seemed muffled. It was as if the atmosphere had grown so thick with pollution that my senses were gradually being snuffed out. As I moved through this surreal state of affairs, I began to wonder if my mother and Judy and Monica were right. Maybe I was a creep. Wasn't that an appropriate name for someone who'd failed on the job and in love and in just about everything else? Or had I missed something more important, in between the specifics of money and position and sex?

$\triangledown$

1 1
FLYING FOOL

I T LOOKED AS THOUGH both gangs had camped out in my room, and when it came to housekeeping one was as untidy as the other: bureau drawers dumped, garbage bags shook out over the table, the striped mattress slit from head to toe, clothes at the bottom of the closet tossed like salad. In the bathroom the cabinet had been torn out of the wall. The chipped sink was clogged with curled Band-aids, sawtoothed razor blades, solidified cherry-flavored cold syrup, and half a bottle of no-brand aspirins. I shook out three tablets and popped them, sticking my head under the faucet and gulping, hoping the barbits would do something for my disposition.

Neither Syd nor Clark had left a strongarm behind to welcome me home. This bothered me. Not that I was hungry for a knuckle sandwich. It just didn't figure. Maybe they thought this trap would be the last place in the world any sane rat would show up. But this was the only room in the world where I wouldn't be turned away. Well, I had my doubts about that too. The deadline for rent kept coming faster than I could earn my keep.

As I was taking a leak, I noticed half an inch of cockroach stretched out on the bristles of my toothbrush, like a fakir on a bed of nails. I didn't shoo it away, having been gone long enough for the roaches to acquire squatters' rights. Zipping up, I checked out the poster of Marilyn Monroe, nude, on the ceiling. To think I had been up against all that silkiness just a few hours ago. Unless my head was making all that up. But even though it made no sense, I felt she was real, and I wondered what had become of her at Goldwine's mansion.

I staggered into my parlour/kitchen/bedroom, which was packed tight: a bed, chest of drawers, portable TV, night table, floor lamp, piles of back issues of the *Squealer* and *Sports Illustrated* on the floor, a couple of tube chairs, a two-burner hot plate, and a portable Remington on a chrome-legged table.

I fit my ass into the sag in the iron-pipe hospital bed, forcing some stuffing out of the slits. On the floor was a copy of *People* magazine, and the cover had a picture of Dustin Hoffman with his arms around Barbra Streisand. The head-line read, "A pair of New York talents expected to dominate Hollywood: Preview of the Academy Awards." Suddenly I knew what I was going to do.

I lifted the phone receiver and listened. Remarkably I got a dial tone. Any day now the service was supposed to be cut off. Still unsure of the day of the week, I dialed Ferdy at home, letting his phone ring and ring and ring, half hoping he wasn't there or was too hung over to pick up. He had enough of his own troubles. But he made the mistake of answering.

"Yeah?"

"Ferdy, it's Igor."

"Stravinsky?"

"Cut it out, Ferdy. What's happening at the *Squealer*?"

"The usual bullshit."

"Can't you be a little more specific?"

"Sure, why not? Lejak claims you hung him up on an assignment . . . something about a fire at a cathouse. Nothing to fill the page-three slot, so he had to throw in an item that'd already run—the one about the snake charmer who got strangled by her boa. Boy, was he pissed."

"It was a fire at the dog pound, and for his information I'm working on a real story for a change."

"Forget it," said Ferdy, yawning in my canal. "Lejak says he's gonna gun you down on sight. This time I believe him."

"Yeah, well, this item's too classy for that rag."

"So what happened to you?"

Ferdy had handed me a segue, but I knew he wouldn't believe me. "Oh, you know how it is. I had a few too many, ended up in this gorgeous barfly's apartment. Earth-mother type. Long red hair. Tits the size of basketballs. Once my head sank into her boobs, I never wanted to come up for air. You know how it is."

"Yeah," said Ferdy, "I know how it is."

"Listen, Ferdy, can you do me a favor?"

The earpiece went dead several seconds. "What kind of favor?"

"I need a few bucks."

"I figured it was that kind of favor. What is it this time? Your mother's lumbago acting up? Your sister wants tap-dancing lessons? Your brother needs a fix?"

"I haven't got a sister. Or a brother."

"That's not what you told me a few months ago!"

"Look, I haven't forgotten the coupla bucks I owe you. Believe me, you'll get it back, every penny."

"Sure, sure, but I'm kinda short on cash right now."

"Ferdy, I wouldn't ask if I didn't need it real bad."

"For what?"

"I'm not sure."

"You're not *sure?*" Ferdy screeched, backing me off the receiver.

"What I mean is it's hard to explain, but I'm up to my neck in trouble. I'm gonna need all the cash I can get."

"You'd better put the bite on another sap."

"I'm desperate, Ferdy," I said desperately.

"Yeah, sure. Somebody gave you a tip on a nag at Belmont."

I had to get his attention. "They're *after* me Ferdy."

"What'd you do? Tap somebody's old lady?" This time he didn't sound nasty.

"You're not gonna believe this, but—"

"You're absolutely right."

"—I was heading home from the office night before last when these hoods pulled up and grabbed me and . . . Look, I don't want to get you mixed up in all this. Honest, I'm in deep trouble. I've got to get out of town. Fast."

When he hesitated, I pressed on. "Soon as I get out of this mess, you'll get it back—all of it."

"Well, I don't know."

"Plus a few bucks extra."

"Hmm."

"You could save my life, Ferdy."

"Cut the crap, Lo*pez*," he said, the accent on the last syllable to get my gall. "How much you talking about?"

"A coupla hundred bucks?"

"A coupla hundred!"

"Unless you got more laying around."

I packed a small cloth grip—boxer drawers with little red targets on them, a pair of cotton socks, a white shirt, worn only twice since the Chinaman had starched it, a green sweater with thin elbows, a new disposable Gillette, a Mickey Spillane paperback, and the passport to my future: the film. The toothbrush I bequeathed to the fakir. Now that strange hands had gone through my bureau drawers and the bugs were using the place as a resort, I didn't feel at home there anymore. I left without locking the door.

On my street, a shabby little rue with more garbage in the gutter than in the cans, white-haired citizens were slowly making their way to the grocery store for a pint of milk and two pounds of potatoes. The city was changing around them quickly and all they could do was get caught in the pinch of shifting neighborhoods. All the way on foot to Ferdy's I couldn't shake the gloom out of my system.

Ferdinand Bagatelle, the *Squealer*'s rewrite man, was sitting on the stoop of his tenement, a ballpoint pen in hand, trying to make sense out of a wad of that nonsense we handed in as copy. His bent-over body was covered by green cotton work trousers and an orange acrylic sweater; a stiffness had set into his broad, thick-featured mug. He was angry at himself for giving in to me.

Without looking up, he said, "Oh, it's you."

"Who'd you expect, Stravinsky?"

"What's the bag for?"

"To carry all the cash you're gonna give me."

"Go ahead, be a wiseass and you won't get a nickel."

"Take it easy, Ferdy. What happened to your sense of humor?"

"I lost it on the way to the bank, Lo*pez*," he said, drawing a folded, smudged white business envelope out of his back pocket. "National Squealer" was imprinted in the upper left corner.

"You're a pal, Ferdy, a real pal." And I meant it.

"I'm a screwball," said Ferdy, and he meant it.

"I'll never forget this," I said.

"You better *not*," he warned, forming a fist as he chucked the envelope at me.

I picked it up and stuffed it into my pocket before he could change his mind.

"Where you going with my money?"

"Hollywood."

"Oh, my God," he moaned, as if facing the fact he'd been taken.

"It's not what you think."

He just kept shaking his head, staring at the copy pages in his lap.

"Pinch Monica's ass for me, will you?"

"When am I gonna see some cash from you?"

"Soon as the heat's off I'll be back, and I expect to have plenty of money on me."

"That's what you always say."

"But this time I mean it."

He started shaking his head again.

"God bless you, Ferdy."

"Screw you," said Ferdy, uplifting his odd body, which looked as if a section had been removed from the middle. He limped up the broken steps with the copy pages rolled up like a white neck in his fist.

Down the subway stairs I lammed and pushed through the turnstile at the drop of my last token, hoping I'd never need another, that I'd end up riding in a limousine on the surface of the earth instead of underground, just like my dad always wanted to do. I jumped into the airport express that stood there with its motor churning. The car was pretty empty, and it gave me a chance to check out the envelope without a pack of pickpockets over my shoulder. The nine-by-four-inch envelope contained a hundred and a half—what a great guy! I figured I'd get seventy-five. There was also a slip of paper that added three previous debts onto the new bill. His handwriting was atrocious, but I got the message. Seems I was into him for almost three hundred smackers. As the train thumped along on an uneven wheel, I wondered why Ferdy had come through and in such a big way once again. Just one of those sad slobs who couldn't say no. Poor Ferdy. It was some kind of curse.

When the train crawled up out of the ground, clicking along the rim of Jamaica Bay, I finally accepted that I was going through with it, actually taking off for Hollywood. I kept glancing around to see if anyone was eyeing me, but everything seemed cool.

After another quarter hour of squealing steel wheels, the train jerked into the station near Kennedy International Airport. It was like arriving in another world. The concrete platforms were stained a lighter gray by the salty air, not blackened by Manhattan pollution, and to see the sky you didn't have to crinkle the back of your neck. The water out in the broad bay looked blue, not brown like the Hudson. Big, graceful white and gray birds flapped their pearly wings over the swaying emerald marshes, as if they actually inhabited the place. It looked as wild as the Brooklyn Botanical Gardens.

Soon I boarded the bus with half a dozen other people and in a few minutes we pulled up alongside the main entrance. I marched into the terminal, which was swarming with souls, cluttered with luggage and soda machines, blinking with signs, and blaring announcements. Not noticing anyone who looked like a stakeout, I headed straight toward the Formica-topped service counters of American Airlines.

If one of Greenstreet's or Gable's boys did materialize and grab me and the film, I decided I would just continue on my pilgrimage—assuming I was still able to walk—step out into Movieland for the first time in my life, collect an autograph or two, visit Disneyland, and then look for work. If I couldn't find a job, I'd write a movie script. But if the gangs didn't latch on to me, I would do my damndest to pawn off the film at NGN. The film had to be worth something to them, having produced it. No way I could deal with the G-boys—didn't trust either of them. Besides, any cash they had was probably Monopoly money.

The cards started falling in my favor. There was a flight in less than half an hour, and I didn't need a reservation. Nor did the pink-faced teller in the too-tight polyester jacket, punching plastic computer keys, lose his mind when I spread the contents of my wallet, piggy bank, and Ferdy's envelope on his counter.

To my surprise I had a nice piece of change left—thank God for price wars! Clutching the cloth sack tightly, I walked from under the high -ribbed ceiling down a sloped corridor and flashed my ticket at the blockade. The only trouble I had was when they were getting ready to run my bag through the scanner to see if I was carrying any bombs. A black security guard with a dry face and billed cap squeezed the sack and said, "What's this?"

"Just a movie reel," I replied quietly, hoping the people behind me wouldn't hear.

"Take it out, please."

I didn't want to take it out and wave it around, so I unzipped the bag and opened it so he could look in.

"Take it out, or it might get ruined by the X ray."

Damn! Hadn't thought of that. A small prank of fate and my future could've been erased. But for all I knew, the heat and dust of time had already ruined the film. Anyway, I quickly pulled the reel out and tucked it inside my jacket under my arm, which made the guard's eyes widen.

"Let's have a look at that, please," he demanded.

Brilliant move, Lo*pez*! I said to myself, slipping it out of my jacket and handing it over. The people behind me started muttering impatiently. The guard pried open the tin, saw that it was only a film, closed the tin, dropped it into the sack, and waved me through with a suspicious look. I hustled into the waiting area, keeping away from other travelers. They must have shared the guard's suspicion, because they kept away from me too. Feeling around in my pockets for a cigarette, I remembered once again I'd given them up. Instead I occupied myself by listening to the announcements of departures. They rattled off a string of exotic places, including Monte Carlo.

At last a block-long aluminum eel, vibrating with low, controlled enthusiasm, rolled up into position outside the loading tunnel. As soon as the door was swung open and the attendant started calling out the seat numbers, I entered the tunnel and went along the covered ramp, past another attendant who stood there greeting passengers. As I entered my row, I realized there was a hostess with orange-colored rayon hair right behind me. "May I see your ticket, please? I don't believe this is your seat. Your number is in the nonsmoking section."

"This is 18C, isn't it?"

"May I see your ticket?"

"Sure, why not." I held it out for her to see.

Looking it over, she saw that I had the right spot, and to make up for her error, I guess, she sank her hooks into my sack. Suddenly we were in a tug-of-war.

"Small bags have to be stored in the compartment overhead," she sniped.

She was stronger than she looked, but I freed it from her pincers. "I've got my heart pills in here," I puffed. "Need them in hand at all times. Doctor's orders." I moved into the seat at the window. The woman in the blue uniform turned on her heel and split. The mood she was in, she must've had a rough transcontinental schedule and not slept for days. Or else she was one of them.

By now passengers were filing into the plane, and I was hemmed in by a jowled lady who raised wire-haired terriers and her wire-haired husband, who manufactured industrial flanges. Both of them spoke as if they had one of his company's products jammed in their mouths. Residing in a split-level in Danbury with a modest kennel out back, they were off to make a surprise visit to their daughter—"a movie thar" in Hollywood.

"Maybe you've hurd of her. Shirley Limpnick?"

"Vaguely," I said, peering into my paperback, trying to get into the exploits of Mike Hammer, who had his left hand in the left cup of the brassiere of a redhead and his right wrapped around a .38 special. But I couldn't help thinking these ding-dongs were in for a shock. Thousands of kids were writing home about how they were cracking the movie business when, in fact, they were the ones being cracked open. These family confidences were offered to me out of the goodness of their Connecticut hearts, which is why they seemed to think they had every right to know all about me. Since I was not inclined to cough up, my face sinking deeper into Mike's adventures, they grew resentful and quiet and finally dozed off into their back issues of *Reader's Digest*.

"May I do something for you, sir?" said another blue uniform from behind, launching me a foot out of my seat.

I wanted to scold her for scaring me out of my hair, but this one was a real time bomb, her long, long legs the color of polished copper pennies. I shook my head to her question, but thought otherwise. When she glanced back from the next row of passengers, I wondered if she was keeping an eye on me or if she just thought I was cute. Certainly I was keeping an eye on her tight skirt. I'd never seen anything like it. As she moved, the dimples in her buttocks actually winked at me.

We were thousands of feet over Des Moines or some such outpost when a man with a befuddled expression and herky-jerky stride came up the aisle and checked me out of the corner of his big, round eyes. If it weren't for his checkered jacket and white sneakers, I would've sworn it was Charlie Chaplin. Tucking my chin into my chest, I realized with horror that up this high there was no place to run and hide.

Soon Chaplin wobbled back down the aisle. I pretended to sleep, and for the rest of the flight I peeked out from under a lash from time to time. Occasionally my neighbors groaned in their dreams of wire-haired flanges. I had to go to the john again; maybe I had diabetes. But I was afraid of attracting attention, so I stayed in my seat and held it in.

All this paranoic behavior was making me feel paranoid, and I tried to calm down by looking out the window at the earth from that special perch. The formations of clouds looked as if they'd been manufactured in a stuffing factory. Through a thin mist I could see the squared-off cuts of farming land, green and tan and brown. It was weird. From up here the world seemed entirely orderly and beautiful, but when you were inside it, close up, it was chaotic and ugly.

12

HOORAY FOR HOLLYWOOD

OVER A SPEAKER BUILT into the false ceiling the pilot announced we were approaching Los Angeles International Airport, so we had to adjust our seats and buckle up. In a few minutes we bounced gently in our cushions as we touched down. The delegation from Danbury began unhooking their safety belts, gathering their magazines and cookies and handbags. As I waited for Shirley Limpnick's parents to step into the aisle, the tune "Hooray for Hollywood" tap-danced in my brain. But the Limpnicks continued to fuss, moving in slow motion, and I began to grow impatient. "I think I'm going to faint," I moaned, weaving slightly for effect. The Connecticut couple glanced my way but continued to fuss. Then I realized the rayon-haired hostess had heard me and was making her way toward us.

"Are you all right, sir?" she said, leaning into our row.

"Oh yes, yes, much better now," I replied, my arm wrapped tightly around my bag.

The hostess disappeared, the Limpnicks began to move, and Chaplin got off ahead of me. I felt relieved. When I reached the exit tunnel, neither of the stewardesses looked at me. But I treated myself to one last wistful gaze at the one with the animated ass. I checked my wrist against the clock on the control tower, which read five after five, and realized I'd racked up a few hours of credit on the flight. Cheating time boosted my confidence, and I adjusted my watch and decided that as soon as I got set up in a room I'd hustle over to NGN. Life was beginning to seem promising again.

Swiftly I moved through the terminal, heading straight for the john. Just as I was pushing the swinging door stamped "Men," Chaplin came hobbling out. Smirking at me, he yanked the bag out of my hands and hopscotched away. I was so surprised, I stood there watching him a few seconds. A cluster of passengers stood right in his path, though, and he got confused, teetered a moment on one leg, and then tripped over a traveling cat cage. The black cat broke loose and shot across the terminal as Chaplin fell on his mustache. My bag leaped out of his hand and slid twenty feet across the polished floor, where it was picked up by a large man in a short gray suit—a plainclothesman. My grandmother could've spotted this one all the way from the Bronx. While the kid who owned the cat went bawling across the terminal in pursuit of Blackie, I sprinted over to the plainclothesman and said, reaching out, "Thanks for getting my bag back. The guy in the checkered jacket tried to rip me off."

Frowning at me, the plainclothes dope opened the bag and looked inside. "If it's yours, tell me what's in it?"

"Aren't you going to catch the thief?"

"Tell me what's in the bag?"

"Drawers, a razor blade, a Mickey Spillane novel."

"What else?"

"What else?"

"You heard me."

"A film case."

Unable to think of any other way to harass me, he

chucked the bag hard into my midsection. Not a pleasant experience on an empty stomach.

"You better hang on to your stuff better, pal."

He had a way of saying "pal" that was like delivering a rabbit punch. I couldn't remember where I'd heard that voice before, but I was glad to be finished with him.

Holding off on the john, I came out under a sky as ambiguous as a movie review. Cabs were hard to come by on Academy Awards weekend in Los Angeles, I figured, after outracing an elderly gent with a cane to the last one at the taxi stand. It took me a while to catch my breath, but out here even the smog smelled good.

On the way to the guts of L.A. the cabbie fed me the plot of a mystery script he was writing about a tea-drinking dick by the name of Hemlock Scholmes. "Sounds vaguely familiar," I said, wondering if Chaplin was in the cab behind us.

"Familiar? There's never been anything like it before or since." What that was supposed to mean I didn't even want to guess. I just wanted to know if it would be smart to try to play one gang against another, using the film as bait. But I decided it would only bring me more grief. Best to do something for myself, entirely on my own.

Even though I'd questioned the originality of his work, the cabbie went on telling me the scenario, which involved murderous bloodhounds on the moors of Scotland. But my mind was in California. So this is Hollywood, I thought. Though the grass was brown and the long palm leaves drooped as if tired, the streets were more spread out, not so claustrophobic as New York, and the low houses on the outskirts reminded me of the bungalows pushed together near the Jersey Shore. The only thing that disturbed me was that I didn't have to go to the bathroom anymore. What was happening to me?

***

I set up headquarters in a picturesquely sleazy motel, The Gold Rush, that looked as if it'd been unloaded from a truck and glued together for the occasion. A clerk with a face like a rubber stamp took me in without so much as snickering at my tie.

I gave him Ferdy's name, but he didn't put it on the books, and pocketed the twenty. I found my way to the ten-by-ten compartment with a piss-in closet, done up with decals of pineapples and hula dancers. First, I kneed the desk chair up under the doorknob, then I squeezed into the john and stood there waving my pecker at the bowl, but I had lost the urge completely. Finally, I fell onto a mattress that seemed to be made of baking dough. Five minutes with my eyes closed was all I needed. . . .

Next thing I knew it was six-thirty-five, and a molten sun was burning a hole through the cheap-paneled back wall. Springing off the gooey bed, I found myself trembling, and I gripped the film case through the cloth sack as if it were a life preserver. The feel of it calmed me. I splashed a couple of palmfuls of chloroform-scented water onto my face, forced a comb through my knotted locks, and popped a stick of Wrigley's spearmint into my jaws. With my toothbrush taken over by the roaches, it was the best I could do.

Though I figured it was too late to reach the party I wanted, I got an outside line anyway, picked up the number of NGN from information, and dialed.

"This is ENNN GEEE ENNN."

"I'd like to speak to the president of the company."

"You mean Mr. Nadler?"

"That's right, honey. Mr. Nadler."

"Just a moment."

Now a husky voice came on. "Mr. Nadler's office."

I pulled away from the receiver, never having gotten used to macho secretaries. "Nadler, please."

"Whom shall I say is calling?"

"Jack Anderson."

"Jack Anderson who?"

"You know, the columnist. Syndicated. Adviser to presidents. Chaperon to princesses. Maker and breaker of governments."

"Oh yes, *Jack* Anderson," said the husky voice. "Well, Mr. Anderson, Mr. Nadler is in a late conference and has left word not to be disturbed."

Now he tells me. "When'll he be finished? I'll call back."

"As soon as his meeting's over, he will be hastening home to prepare to attend the Academy Awards."

"This is a matter of life and death."

"Sorry, Mr. Anderson."

"Nadler'll give you a raise for this."

"Sorry, Mr. Anderson."

"Go suck an egg." I hung up loudly. But it was obvious I had to get over to NGN quickly.

I grabbed my bag, locked the door, and hustled up to the registration desk. The clerk looked at me head-on for the first time. He had oily, selfish eyes that would rather have been squinting at racing forms than at my wasted face. "I wonder if you could tell me where NGN is located," I said.

"Sure I could."

Maybe he could, but he didn't. The thick-lidded lad sat there displaying some chipped yellow teeth, so I shook out a copy of George Washington's wig over his palm. All he did was yawn, the back of his claw still stuck in the counter.

With a limited stake to my name, I grabbed my buck out of his mitt—surprising him mightily—and kept the cloth sack under my wing as I bolted that fun house of quarter-inch paneling.

Took ten minutes to collar a cab. The driver, a character with seventy-year-old skin and twenty-year-old, wavy brown hair, a kind of updated Ramon Novarro, said, "Where to, bub?"

"NGN."

The man shrugged, drove away from the curb with a jerk. Within less than a block he started cruising as slowly as a tour bus.

"See that marble building over there?" he said. "That's where Gloria Swanson used to throw fabulous parties in her heyday."

"Don't you know where NGN is?"

"You bet your life, bub." But the scrap-heap Dodge kept rolling along just slowly enough to get caught at every light.

"Frank Sinatra keeps a suite of rooms in that hotel just to change his tie when he's downtown on business."

"Step on it, will you? NGN'll be closing soon."

"Haven't had a traffic summons in forty years," he informed me. "No percentage in starting now."

Maybe he smelled the Bronx on my jacket and was taking me for a ride, but I couldn't bail out. I might not've been able to latch on to another cab. At last he confessed he was rewriting *The Bad Seed* as a musical comedy.

"I'm gonna lose out on a big deal!" I nearly screamed.

"Don't worry, bub. I got this hunch we are *both* going to strike it rich."

Twenty minutes later we pulled up before a perfectly square, glassy-faced construction with all the warmth of an insurance company headquarters in Hartford. I had a feeling my motel was around the corner. But I couldn't prove it. The meter read thirteen bucks! Not that it mattered—I'd never intended to pay anyway. I leaped out of the cab and took off. The driver got out and ran after me. Pretty long strides for an aging screenwriter! Having done a little broken-field running in the alleys of the South Bronx, though, I left him in the smog.

"Stop that man!" he shouted, but people are as blasé—as numb—in Hollywood as they are in New York, and they just went on about their business.

Toward the front revolving doors spinning with people in flowery shirts and pastel slacks and short-shorts, I sprinted. The uniformed guard out in the plaza didn't even glance my way as I approached. Suddenly I bashed head-on into Marilyn Monroe. She seemed to bounce off me like a balloon.

"What're you doing here?" I hollered.

"Aren't you glad to see me?" she said, taking me by the hand and leading me to the curb. Before I could protest, she shoved me into the open door and seat of an English roadster, blood red, which was idling in an illegal zone. She skipped to the other side of the car, jumped in, knocked it into gear, and we were on our way.

"Stop the car! I've got an important appointment."

"Are you trying to sell the film to NGN?"

My whole life would be different if only I weren't so transparent. "How did you know I was here?" I demanded.

"After waiting for you at the Century Plaza," she puffed as we peeled along the pavement, "I took a chance on coming here—couldn't think of any other place you might go. You angry at me or something?"

"You're in cahoots with someone, I just don't know who."

"I'm in cahoots with you, honey."

"Yeah, sure."

A small pink hand she set on my knee, just like Judy Plane, and she flickered those mascaraed eyelashes at me. "What do you think we're going to do right now?"

"Promises, promises."

After a minute or two of flying down the streets, she

glanced at my sack and asked, "Do you have the film with you?"

She'd caught me flatfooted again, but I countered by asking her a question. "What makes everyone think I have the film?"

"You *told* me you had it stashed in Goldwine's."

"I lied."

"I don't think so. Why else would you be here?"

"To watch the Lakers lose a game for a change."

Her being at NGN was too much of a coincidence, but that's the way things happened in the movies. Besides, I was a guy who needed an accomplice, preferably a sexy one. I went along for the ride. Maybe I could catch up with Nadler later. As we sped past lights down the boulevard, I noticed a young tanned couple in a Jeep alongside us staring at the driver's seat in the roadster with wide eyes.

13

MAKIN' OUT

THE AIR WAS STALE. Dead. A pair of black walnut chairs tightly wrapped in blue velvet, with gold-studded armrests, flanked the entranceway like a pair of sphinxes guarding the gates of hell. The corridor was short, but the walls curved open into a space that was more an area than a room, and it had obviously been designed for pleasure. The entire ceiling was covered with a vast sheet of lavender silk that must've kept several million silkworms busy for years. Along the bay window hung a waterfall of silvery braids. A fruit bowl hacked out of onyx, fruitless, was centered on a crystal table. The bar at the other end was also in crystal, with a pricey-looking sound system built into its facade. Rugs made of hair lined the walls, and fur-wrapped cushions cluttered the floors. Between the cushions I could see a room-sized painting of a Roman orgy in full swing, complete with pillars and pools and perversities.

"You confuse the hell out of me."

Marilyn kicked off one red patent-leather shoe, then the other, bringing her closer to earth. "Why? I'm easy as apple pie," she said. "All boobs, no brains."

The flash of teeth, the slitted eyes were not remotely related to the pouts and giggles she'd been dishing out all day.

"You've got plenty more than that going for you."

"Why, thank you, sir," she said with a southern lilt, mocking me.

"I just wish I knew whose side you're on."

This time her tone came by way of L.A. "Right now, honey, all you need to know is you're a man and I'm a woman."

What I really wanted to know was whether she was a dream or a nightmare.

Marilyn did a kind of snake dance to shimmy out of her glossy, 1950s-length flair dress. The garment was a pile of gold dust at her feet, and she stood out in the soft light in pale panties, pure and brilliant, a perfect pearl without the half-shell. Skin that looked reasonably genuine was drawn smoothly over her big bones. Then she unhooked the bra, relieving the nylon of its awesome burden, and I gasped as if I'd been relieved of the pressure in my groin. What picturesque tits!

At last she slithered the pinch of silk off her hips and down her legs, flicking it over her shoulder as if for good luck, and I now knew for certain she was a bleached blond. By the time she fluffed up the spun flax on her head with her silver-tipped fingernails, all I could do was make the sign of the cross.

"Get indecent, already."

For the first time in years I felt shy, and I stood as stiff and stupid as a traffic light, blinking at her.

"Come on, I want to try on that gorgeous body of yours."

Her calling my body gorgeous was like Gary Cooper calling Mickey Rooney "Daddy Long Legs." With my trousers extended in homage, clutching the cloth sack to my chest, I muttered, "Are you trying to tell me you're interested in my physical and mental salvation and not *Escape to Monte Carlo*?"

"I want you *and* the film," she said, the gleaming topaz in her sockets forcing me to avoid her eyes. Instead my eyes grazed over the balance of arcs and slopes and swells of her body, and I wondered if this meant she was selling her ass to me for the film.

Marilyn squeaked, pressed herself against me, and set on my lips a kiss that tasted as if a butterscotch Life-Saver had just melted in her mouth.

Somehow I managed to strip down to my bag of human parts without letting go of the cloth sack. Standing in the indirect lavender glow from overhead, I was wishing there would be a blackout so she wouldn't be able to see the contrast between what she was giving and what she was getting: my turned-in feet, the rib cage sticking out, the little paunch containing the only fat on my body. And so she couldn't laugh at what I had connected to my crotch, I kept my skivvies on.

"What macho legs you have," said Marilyn.

I looked at the doorknobs I had for knees. They weren't even a good match.

Her buttocks jiggled as she moved deeper into the penthouse, past the crystal bar and the white marble sculpture of a man and a woman, naked, locked in an embrace that would last forever. I had a strong feeling I'd seen the sculpture in a museum. In the middle of the room she dropped down onto a foot-thick cushion that had to have been imported from an Arabian harem. There she sat, full and fine, the Sultan's latest acquisition. "Pour me a drink, baby. A big one."

Though I knew I should've been heading back to NGN, trying to piece together a future—running for my life—I moved to the bar, set my sack down carefully behind it, and said, "What kind of booze blows up your skirt?"

"Bourbon—straight up," she said without a blink.

I was beginning to think Marilyn Monroe really was going

to come across, and it made me nervous enough to really appreciate some liquor. The bar stock was ample and various, from the cheap American rotgut to the fancy foreign stuff. With the trade deficit getting worse every day, I went for the domestic and poured a pair of triples. Nature had worked earnestly, if not very long, to produce the stuff. No sense letting it evaporate.

I took a jolt and moved toward her, carefully balancing the thick whiskey-sour glasses. Marilyn looked impatient as a thirty-year-old virgin as she reached up for the drink. She had taken a hefty belt by the time I hit the cushion. Not very gracefully I landed, spilling some of the bourbon on my leg.

"Don't waste a drop!" she cried, leaning down and licking the wet spot off my thigh.

My leg jerking involuntarily, I sipped my drink, watching in awe as she knocked off the rest of her triple in one neat gulp.

Marilyn sighed to let the burning in her throat subside, I guess, then set her glass on a small crystal caddy just within reach of her outstretched arm. Now she lifted one of the cushions, exposing a panel of switches and dials set down into the floor. After she had twisted and flipped a couple of them, the stereo began to roll some soft, lush, mildly classical sounds into the area—my guess is Debussy—and the silk ceiling began to undulate in time with the music.

"Man, if we could turn the minds of these movie moguls over to the problems of poverty instead of the playthings of pleasure, we'd probably be able to eliminate social injustice."

It was more of my insecure chatter to keep me from facing up to her sexual offerings. But Marilyn wasn't paying attention to me. She lay back on the cushions, spreading out her body before me. She was like a wet dream come to life. Her small porcelain foot drew up toward her dimpled kneecap, creating a figure four with her legs. A glaze had coated her eyes, and her skin glimmered as if it were too hot to touch. But that's not why I kept my hands to myself. I was afraid of her, of what would happen to a member of the audience reaching out for the screen. Weren't there laws against that sort of thing? And then there was the matter of our respective states of being. I was afraid that if I plugged into her, somehow it would make me one of them.

Inspecting the orgy painting on the floor, I said, "What is this joint?"

"Goldwine's private palace of sin. Downtown branch."

"Looks like two different people lived in Goldwine's places in New York and California."

"You should see the castle he built on a hill outside Palm Beach."

"How lucky for you to have a passkey to all his hot spots."

Her look answered part of my implied question, and her lips told me the rest. "When I was new in the business, trying to get my break, Goldwine promised me something—a part that would've started my career off with a bang. The kind of part that would've made the world realize I was more than tits and ass."

"What was it, *War and Piece*?"

As if embarrassed, she coughed lightly before speaking. "He told me he was going to remake *Gone With the Wind*—an ever bigger and more lavish production. He swore that I would be his Scarlet O'Hara. He was going to rebuild Atlanta stick by stick and burn it to the ground . . . just for me. Vivien Leigh was furious and threatened to sue NGN, but Goldwine said he didn't care, as long as it made me happy. I was only a kid. I believed him."

No way could I visualize a magnolia in Marilyn's teeth.

Suddenly she got up and pranced to the bar, where she poured herself another deep dose of bourbon. I noticed there were creases under her behind.

"Were you in New York when Goldwine was . . .?"

Marilyn flicked those eyes on me, only now they'd softened into velvet. "Are you asking me if I know anything about his death?"

"I only wondered if you had any theories."

"No theories. I know who killed him."

"Just like that, you know?"

"Let's just say I saw it happen."

"Why didn't you tell the police or something?" I said, wondering if that were as easy as it sounded.

"They wouldn't have listened to me. Besides, I killed the dirty bastard myself."

"What! You? I find that pretty hard to believe."

"Well, you'd better try a little harder," she said with a certain defiance.

The air got stuck in my throat a moment. "You're not capable of anything like that, Marilyn. You're gentle. You're warm. You're a symbol of love."

"Iggy, listen to me. I blasted Stan Goldwine to kingdom come."

I watched her take a swallow, trying to get the idea of her as a murderess to sit still in my head. Maybe I was reluctant to accept it because she had suddenly pulled the chain on the mystery, and my career as a detective was going right down the drain.

"And I'd do it again and again."

The way everybody was getting up out of their graves and walking around, I thought, she just might have to. "Jezuz, I know you must've been disappointed about not getting that role," I said, "but that promise was broken years ago, when you were still . . ."—I was going to say "alive" but decided to avoid the subject out of respect for the dead—"a kid."

"For years I watched him lie to other women, and other

producers pulled the same trash on me. I guess it got to be too much, and then I got a little high one night, and he tried to pull another line on me. I let him have it. But I didn't do it for me, Iggy, not just for me." A touch of maudlin tipsiness had slipped into her voice. No longer hanging on to her glass, Marilyn moved back to the cushions and sank down beside me. I could feel the warmth radiating off her skin. Back in New York her skin had felt cool. Was she getting warmer, or was I getting cooler? "I did it for all those kids who were having their ups and downs, trying to break into the business. And I did it for all those fading performers who went to him for help. I did it for the women of America."

I wondered how Shirley Limpnick, the Connecticut comet, was faring on the casting couches of Hollywood.

"I did it as a warning to every man who ever made promises to a woman in Hollywood and New York and Vegas." Her voice was slurred. "By shooting Goldwine I was trying to kill the men who had the power to keep their promises but who didn't. The men who use women physically and mentally."

With movies like *How to Marry a Millionaire* and *Gentleman Prefer Blondes* under her garter belt, Marilyn didn't seem like good feminist material.

"Some men can only be stopped with violence."

If ghosts were going around murdering off the living, no wonder there were so many unsolved murders. But what a story! "Monroe Bumps Off Goldwine Over Broken Movie Promise." Who would buy it? Certainly not the *News*. Not even the *Squealer* would touch it.

Under the soft undulations of the silk ceiling I lay, the controlled passion of the music going right to my groin. I was hip to hip with a cold-blooded, vengeful, blond widow spider. But I didn't feel turned off by her—if possible, I got harder: so hard I thought my pecker was going to split like an overboiled hot dog. A woman passionate enough to blow away a big shot like that had to be a wicked screw. Yet I still felt too chicken to touch her.

"What happened when you and I were at Goldwine's in New York?" I said, working hard to avoid looking at her huge nipples. "I was worried about you after you went downstairs."

"I can take care of myself."

"Since I didn't know if you were with Gable's or Syd's gang, I couldn't figure out what was going on."

She didn't bite.

"I heard a gunshot. . . ."

As if telling the time of day, she said, "That pistol-happy Wayne plugged me," and with the palm of her hand she shoved her right breast aside, revealing a small black hole. "That's all I need—another hole in my body."

Either she was the greatest actress of all time, or the fabulous Miss MM really *was* hot for me, dripping with sex as she rolled over on top of me, having gotten "tired of all this talk, talk, talk." She was light as meringue, and panting like an iron lung. Her satiny arms wound around me and her red mouth sucked in my lips, and then she wrapped her soft legs around my waist and began to thrust her body toward me to the rhythms of Debussy.

Now we began bouncing on the furry cushions like kids on a trampoline. But I was so long overdue that a monstrous pain began wrenching my groin, as if someone were standing on my nuts. My head was pulsing, my feet tingling, my hands producing a thick oil.

At last I lost all my fears somewhere in the madness of my need—I was going to make it with Monroe if it killed me. My hips began hammering at her crotch, but I kept missing, or so it seemed in the tangle of our bodies. I pushed her legs open wider to get a better aim and started hammering again. Her blond hair splashed with each stroke. Now Marilyn started laughing hysterically. Not sure how to take it, I was so crazy by this time that I just kept jabbing away, and even though I'm not really sure if I actually hooked up with her, my limbs rumbled and my crotch quaked. Suddenly my mind squirted out of my skull and my soul dribbled out of my body. . . .

When I woke up she was gone, and I sat up on the cushions, Indian-style, trying to figure out whether I had scored or not. If I had, the usual signs were missing. Particularly I missed the excruciating pleasure during and the great sense of relief after. I didn't feel like singing in the bathtub or eating a pastrami on rye or even lighting up a Camel. I just felt subdued. If I had succeeded in making it with her, it was obvious the experience wasn't the same with one of them, not any more satisfying than witnessing sex on a movie screen.

I sat there with my mind drifting in this direction until I realized I was counting the ashtrays—eight, and all made of marble. It was one of those places in which the ashtrays were whisked away and returned between every flick of the cigarette. But the butlers were gone, gone to graveyards every one.

There was something that had to be done, I sensed, somewhere to go, someone to see. What and where and who it was, I couldn't say. I just sat there yawning, stretching, knuckling my eyesockets. When I noticed the gold-rimmed starburst on the wall—eighteen to eight—the cobwebs snapped.

I shot up and bounded over the pillows in my nakedness to the bar. My cloth sack lay exactly where I'd dropped it. To my astonishment the film was still in it. Marilyn continued to confuse me.

In the john the round walls were satin-quilted like a
padded cell for millionaires. I splashed rusty water on my
face. Gradually the nervous energy began to pump through
my body, and my talent for worry resurfaced. I worried about
the lack of feeling in my hands, about the neighborhood my
mother had moved to, about where Marilyn had gone, and
especially about the film's losing its value like an over-
inflated stock. What else could I do but look for Nadler at
the Academy Awards? Unfortunately, Charlton Heston had
neglected to mail me an invitation.

From the bedroom closet that spanned the room I borrowed a hat—one of those plumed, sweep-rimmed jobs out
of *The Three Musketeers*, plus a long purple cape. Stuff left
over from a Goldwine movie, party, romance—all three
probably. In the dressing salon attached to the john I found
a cabinet with a full stock of cosmetics. Guess he wanted
his girls to look just right before he went in for the kill. I
penciled in a mustache, darkened my brows, extended my
sideburns. In Topeka I would've stood out like a Forty-second Street pimp at a church bazaar. In Hollywood I figured
to blend in like another Toyota on the freeway. Peeking out
into the hallway, I strode to the elevator—a kind of rehearsal
for my entrance at the Awards, if I could get that far. It
occurred to me that the desire to dress up like someone else
was contagious out here.

With the film stuffed in the front of my pants, I slipped
out the delivery door of the green glass tower to avoid the
doorman. On the other hand, he was probably working over
dialogue for his movie script and wouldn't have noticed me
anyway. Racing down a cab took a few minutes, and when
I dropped into the back seat, the film popped out of my pants.
"Century Plaza!"

"Not going to be easy tonight," said the female cabbie,

who was wearing a leather aviator's cap with the goggles drawn down over her eyes.

We rolled between a row of chunky buildings whose stucco was crumbling like old, dried makeup.

"Are you a celeb?"

"Yes, please get me there on time."

"I don't recognize you. What's your name?"

"You wouldn't know it. My pictures are all the rage in Europe."

"Oh, you must be one of those American directors who went to Italy to make westerns."

"Yup."

Now the cabbie started cutting sharply in and out of the road hogs like a stunt driver. She didn't strike me as one of them, but you can't judge a ghost by its makeup.

The cabbie looked back and said, "I'm in the movies, too." Before I could shut her up with another outrageous lie, she started telling me about this audition she'd gone to for a new horror movie, *The Attack of the Mutant Aphids*. "Spent all day in the library studying aphids. Did you know the males have wings but the females don't? From an acting point of view, it makes quite a difference."

I was glad to meet someone in L.A. at last who didn't claim to be a scriptwriter. But she should have been looking where she was going—*slam-bang* we climbed up the sloped tailgate of a customized hotrod hammered out of a prewar hearse. The engine gulped and failed. I had ricocheted off the back of the front seat and was banged up and felt woozy. More or less unruffled by the crash, the cabbie climbed out and strutted over the patch of graveled shoulder, where the hearse with the painted orange flames sat dented and smoking. The other cars were honking, but the motorists didn't seem angry so much as gleeful. They loved an accident in this town, where people did most of their living and dying behind the steering wheel, where everything rolled merrily along like a movie scenario.

While the short-haired cabbie and the square-haired kid were checking out the damage, I reorganized my arms and legs and shook myself out of the hunk of junk. Sore spots stood out on me like welts on a boxer's body after ten rounds. Just then I spotted a red roadster flash by, top down, being driven by a woman with a full flow of blondness. Beside her was a man with greasy dark hair combed back.

All I had to do was follow the crowd. It was six minutes to eight when I reached the Century Plaza, and it was wild as that New York ticker-tape parade for the Mets. People were yards deep behind police barriers, and they were cheering as if it were the seventh game of the World Series. Inspired by the excitement, I began elbowing into the mobs, crying out, "Make way for the Count! Make way for the Count!" Impressed by my plumes and cape, I guess, they actually opened up for me. But I was afraid my sideburns were smudging, so I pulled the brim of my hat lower and barged ahead.

Under a wooden barrier I ducked without being spotted by the police. The flow of invited guests carried me toward the front entrance as if I were a new-wave director, eccentric but brilliant. Cops were everywhere—in vehicles and patrolling the barriers. Spotlights were splashing back and forth across the throng. Thousands of people were cheering, standing on their toes to gobble up the glamour, as though it would add instant beatification to their feeble lives.

To my astonishment I found myself tucked in between Elizabeth Taylor and Johnny Carson, both of whom looked younger than in their pictures: must've gone through a Hollywood face factory. Poor Liz had lost yet another millionaire husband, but she was holding up well. And Johnny was checking out a bevvy of starlets to his right. Just ahead of me were Peter Falk, Sidney Poitier, Norman Mailer, and Joe DiMaggio. The ballplayer never seemed to age! I wondered if Joe D would've minded my playing around with his ex. I would've liked to discuss her with him—the way two men who have been married to the same woman like to do. But there was no time for social tea.

Behind me, more of the same—the biggies, the hotshots, the superstars. It was name droppers heaven. But I was going to give myself away if I kept staring at them like a fan, so I grinned defiantly and hoofed ahead. You've got to behave like a star before people can become intimidated enough to treat you like one.

On a platform in the open plaza the network cameras were swiveling, the commentators trying their damndest to identify me for their millions of viewers. Worldwide! But subject matter was plentiful, and so the cameras were quickly punched away to the latest arrivals, stepping out of their lean black limos, smiling the smiles of the biggest dreamers of all in a land of dreamers.

Just before the entranceway, Liz, Johnny, and I moved up close behind a tall, silver-haired couple in tux and gown. I wondered if they were the Nadlers. Suddenly—or so it seemed—I was swept on the energy of Taylor and Carson into the lobby of the Century, where they honored the kings and queens of celluloid. No one asked me to prove I belonged, or existed.

$\triangledown$

14
CAUGHT IN THE ACT

THE FOYER OF THE Century Plaza was high, wide, and agleam, and the population was aglitter. I hadn't seen that many jewels since I'd stood at the windows of Tiffany's, fantasizing a holdup. Nearby, Lauren Bacall wore earrings that looked like ice cubes. Beside her stood Jane Russell, a spray of rubies at her neck. Both were smiling stiffly, as though they didn't really like standing next to each other. Lauren's sophisticated attractiveness had crumpled, and Jane's great legs had turned to balusters. But once they were gone, apparently they would revert back to their prime anyway. Not a bad deal, unless you hadn't had a prime.

I considered asking Bacall and Russell if they would point Nadler out to me. But I felt intimidated. Besides, I didn't want them to get a good look at my makeup. With all these big names milling around, Igor Lopes might as well have been standing on the planet Venus. That's how distant, how alone I felt. All of them were chatting furiously in their own circles, all part of the sparkle, no one even glancing in my direction. Not until a man wearing a satin maroon turban, with a thin coat of greenish grease smeared over his face, peered straight into my eyeballs. My backbone turned to stone.

Through the crowd toward a staircase that flowed down

off the main runway I went. On the lower level I cut across a lounge area where some vaguely familiar faces were poking cigarettes into their faces. The cloud of cancerous smoke smelled wonderful. I shouldered through a doorway, down another flight of concrete stairs, plunging into the cata-combs of the Century Plaza, where all the pipes and wires that kept this massive illusion operating were stashed out of sight of polite eyes. I came across a workers' washroom, dashed up to a sink, and in a couple of minutes scrubbed the gunk off my face.

Outside the washroom was a row of army-green metal lockers lined against the cinder block wall. Finding one of them unlocked, I took off my cape and hat, and helped myself to a big pair of overalls, pulling them on over my jacket and trousers. I also snatched a baseball cap, which I pulled down over my eyes, and slipped the film reel into the overalls. Then I poked my way down the dim passage. Just as I reached the freight elevator the double steel doors opened and there stood a balding runt in the same kind of overalls as me, one foot up on a cardboard box. He looked over my uniform kind of slowly: everybody wanted to get into the act of playing detective.

"Going up?" he said.

"To the top," I replied, getting in.

As the cables drew us up, he got nosey. "You new here?"

"Yeah, just started Monday."

"Who you working with?"

Without flinching, I said, "Joe." Whenever pressed for a name, you can never go wrong with Joe.

"Joe?"

Before he could start thinking too much, I started talking. "Guess I'll get to see a lot of movie stars on this job."

"Maybe."

"And the hotshots—the guys who run the big movie companies. Like this guy Nadler—the head of NGN. You must've seen him around."

"Nadler? Never heard of him. Don't tell me you took this job looking for a break in the movies."

"Sort of. What about you—what kind of script are you writing?"

"A suspense thriller about this life insurance broker who bumps off his clients to get even with the company."

"Sounds like a natural."

The elevator stopped, and I got out. A series of metal ramps and platforms with guardrails overlooked a huge cutout in the floor. The man in the overalls hoisted the box and set it outside the elevator, then got back in. "Good luck," he said.

"Same to you. We'll need it." I felt lucky to have shaken him off that easily.

As I passed from one side of the building to the other, I could see the stage twenty-five or thirty feet below. Along the outer perimeter of the ramps were several storage and work areas, including a row of terminal boxes and levers that must've controlled stage lights and the movement of backdrops. Farther along the ramp I spotted another guy in overalls, bent over, bolting cable along the beam. Before he could turn and spot me I stepped behind a black canvas-covered frame that was hanging from a pair of steel cables.

The orchestra was warming up. It sounded like a TV studio band—the cheap brilliance of too many trumpets and not enough trombones. As the sounds of the orchestra began to take a hummable shape, the workman finished up and took his toolbox with him. Once he disappeared down the metal stairs, I came out of hiding.

The clamorous noise of the celebrity-nuggeted audience filed down to a low, vibrating hum of anticipation. A crewman raced across the far corner of the stage below me, and then I heard the raucous laugh of Phyllis Diller. Moving closer to the rail at the edge of the ramp, I saw Diller standing with Bob Hope behind the curtains. She was wearing a yellow sequined miniskirt, and he had on a tan business-man's suit with a purple carnation in his lapel.

A swell of applause rose up out of the audience, but it sure as hell wasn't for me. I'd come a long way, and now it looked as though I was stymied. Somewhere in the crowd down-stairs was the one person who might be able to turn my life around. Yet there was a social ocean between us, plus I didn't even know what he looked like. And tomorrow might be too late. If I didn't get rid of the film right away, the celluloid gangs would catch up to me and take it away. And even more unsettling was the thought that maybe the film had already been ruined by New York's deadly atmosphere. I wondered why I had come to California at all.

A flurry of voices broke behind me. Quickly I ducked into a storage closet jammed with buckets of dried paint. Crisp as a drumstick tapping a cymbal, I could hear their feet slapping along the metal ramp. I wondered if it was more workmen, or maybe Syd's boys had been tipped off by the greasy face in the turban. It turned out to be Gable and Robinson, and they were arguing—only a lot hotter now.

"If somebody'd listened to me long ago," snapped Edward G., "we'd be back in New York watching the Awards on TV, not sneaking around out here."

"Who needs New York? Who needs TV? This is where the action is."

"You don't even know if Syd's got the film."

"Look," said Gable, "I've got a hunch, okay?"

"Yeah, ever since you played a reporter you've been getting lots of hunches."

"Why don't you just shut up and listen for a change? All we have to do is sit pretty and wait for Syd to show up at the projection room. If he doesn't, we can go back east and rest a lot easier. But if he does show up, we'll be in a good spot to stop him from showing that film."

"What if they have a projector rigged somewhere else?" said Robinson.

"Lombard and Niven are searching the Plaza top to bottom. What more can I do?"

Their voices died out as they moved down toward the far end of the building. I decided to get off that level quickly and find my way back stage if I could. Maybe someone down there could point out Nadler to me. But it occurred to me that even if I could locate him, Nadler might not want to be bothered with the likes of me on a night like this. How could I be sure for that matter that NGN would want to lay out a bundle for *Escape to Monte Carlo* when they probably had money troubles like the rest of the business? My options seemed to be running out like dirty water in a bathtub, and it was beginning to look as though I might come up empty-handed once again.

Stepping out of the closet, I found myself nose to nose with Joan Crawford, -fixed up the way a dame should be fixed up on Academy Awards night. Her hair was stacked up—a chocolate ice cream sundae, and her Oriental silk wrap-around clung to her hips like Saran wrap. Only thing that didn't go with her outfit was the blue steel rod she whipped out of her rhinestone-studded evening purse.

"Spence!" she called over her shoulder. "Look what I caught crawling around up here." Far down the platform I saw Spencer Tracy stop, turn and start swaying toward us like a big overgrown kid, smiling keenly between his curly hair and black bowtie.

"Why if it isn't the greasy little reporter," said Tracy, frisking me kind of roughly.

"Take it easy, will you?"

"What have we here?" said Spencer, finding the disk in the overalls.

"Let's not get personal," I said, backing off.

"Stand right where you are," ordered Crawford.

Without asking my permission, Tracy unzipped the side of the overalls, reached inside, and plucked out the film reel.

"Holy smokes!" said Tracy.

"We've got it!" cried Crawford. "We've got it!"

"Quick. Let's find Clark and Edward," said Spencer, jogging toward the far end of the ramp with the film under his flipper.

"What should I do about *this*?" she said, shaking the nozzle in my direction.

"We don't need him anymore," he called back over his shoulder.

Joan considered me a moment, then tucked the rod away, as if afraid a shot might be heard. "So long, you poor sap," she said, scurrying after Tracy. One more movie cliché, I thought, and I'd be dead anyway from overexposure.

As I was schlepping down the stairs, brooding about my lousy, apparently interminable bad luck, Eric von Stroheim came stomping up them.

"Ya!" he grunted, charging me. I stood as stiff as if a strange dog had rushed me. He started frisking me.

"This is getting monotonous."

"You gif feelm to Gaple?"

"No, I didn't gif it to Gaple—Tracy and Crawford *took* it."

Grabbing me by the overall straps, he demanded, "How long 'go you gif feelm to Gaple?"

"Two minutes," I rasped, freeing myself from his grip.

Kong's eyes brightened.

"They're all over at the projection room right now," I said, figuring that information was worth something, such as a head start down the stairs.

Then I heard more thunder coming up the stairs. Syd's bulk filled the stairwell. "The reporter!" he exclaimed. "*Excellent.*"

"Gaple's got feelm," said von Stroheim gravely.

Syd stared at me with bulls eyes in his sockets.

"I'm not playing ball with them," I said sincerely.

Syd didn't believe me, but his goon said, "We haf to hurry before they destroy feelm."

Syd seemed all the fatter in the shadows as he pounded up the stairs. King Kong was at my heels, pushing me in the same direction.

Down on the stage I could hear Charlton Heston's voice rising above the hum of the audience. "And now, it is my great pleasure and privilege to present, Mr. Comedy himself, Ba-ahb Ho-ope!" As the orchestra blared a few riffs of "Thanks for the Memories," the three of us moved along the length of the building past the cables and hardware they used to create illusions on stage. Below, the audience exploded with appreciation.

"The Academy Awards used to be such a fashionable affair." Hope chuckled. "How come no one got dressed up for the occasion? Where's your jeans and T-shirts? . . ."

When we reached the swinging door that led to the area surrounding the projection booth, I could hear the loud voices of Gable, Robinson, Wayne, and Crawford. Strange. They had gotten what they'd come for and yet they still sounded angry. Seemed like they were never satisfied.

"It's now or never," Syd whispered.

Peeking through the crack between the swinging door, Eric said, "We're much outnumbered."

The two of them looked at me.

"Don't look at *me*," I said.

Syd shook his head slowly. "Typical. Opportunity knocks on your door, and you turn away. Precisely the reason you can never improve your situation."

I felt defensive. "Why should I help you after ducking your bullets all day?"

"Simply because it is in your best interests."

"Like hell. I'll only end up getting trampled to death in between the gangs."

"You're already half dead," Syd whispered with a low gush of earnestness that shocked me.

I'd been suspecting something was wrong with me for quite a while, but I hadn't thought it was quite that far gone. Out of habit I defended my mortality. "I can still bleed, can't I?"

"Considering the life you've been living," he said, "I doubt it. Don't you see? You're in the same predicament as Eric and me. You're losing more and more of your ties to the real world."

Even if he was right, my life, such as it was, still had value to me. "If I'm gonna get kicked around, I want money."

"I shall see that you get it," he said, pushing me through the swinging doors before I could ask how much.

$\triangledown$

15
PIE IN THE EYE

THE SHIFTS IN MY loyalty were about as swift as those in
the movies, and I was just as surprised by my new role as
Gable's gang was when my partners smothered Edward G.
and Clark with their bodies. That left big John Wayne, the
cowpoke, and Joan Crawford, the slowpoke, for me. Before I
could talk it over with them I was tackled from behind by
Spencer Tracy, who cried, "Oh no, you don't."

"Sydney!" shouted Clark, "listen to me!" But Syd took a
swipe at him, so Gable led with a clean right cross in the
vicinity of the boss's temple. Syd feinted to his right and
flicked a sharp chop to Clark's chin, sending his squared-off
mustache sprawling backwards over a table. Pretty fancy
footwork for a behemoth.

Wayne forgot about me and grabbed Eric with both hands
around the neck. But the bald bomber jabbed his elbow in
Wayne's gut and Duke bounced off the wall like a pink
Spaulding ball. Clark and Edward G. teamed up and bowled
Syd over with their shoulders, and they pinned him to the
floor. All that was missing was the popcorn.

Lon Chaney, Jr., in his tight black suit, came rushing
through the swinging doors and jumped on Edward G's back.
Still smoking a cigar, the little man jerked forward and

flipped him headfirst onto the floor. Wayne stomped on Chaney's neck, and that angered me. I was used to seeing the guys in the black hats, not the ones in white hats, kick a man when he was down.

Stupidly I climbed out from under the table and jumped the Duke from behind. He didn't go down, his momentum carrying him forward with me on his back. As I hacked at his glossy neck, he slammed me into the wall. I dropped like a bag of garbage. He was about to unload his size-fifteen boot on my head when I grabbed his leg and twisted. Down he went. "Tim-ber!"

While I was looking around for the film, Clark was shouting something about making a big mistake. Frustrated that no one would listen to him, Gable came romping after me. "You filthy dog!"

I scrambled to my feet and sprinted toward the door. But Edward G. caught me with a bollo punch alongside the ear, and I went over like an empty beer can. Behind me I heard a piece of furniture shatter against a wall.

Staggering to my feet, rubbing my head, I saw something I never want to see again, though I'd seen it happen on the screen many times. Chaney sat on the floor grimacing, the long black hairs popping out on his face. In a minute or two he was growling, crawling on all fours, and covered with fur. Guess there was a full moon out. Chills shot down to my toes.

The wolf sprang after Crawford. I would've liked to take a bite out of that one myself. But she was quick with the hands and had the pistol aimed point-blank and fired, winging the Wolfman, who bolted through the door yelping all the way. Must've been a silver bullet.

Suddenly I spotted the film case under a table, and I crawled in that general direction. Crawford tried to step on my hand, so I shot it up her dress.

"You pig!" she squealed, dropping the pistol in surprise.

Eric stomped toward Crawford, who swung around and kneed him in the nuts. What great knees! Eric doubled over and Tracy cracked him over the cranium with the leg of a table. The big ape merely scratched his head. But we were losing the battle and maybe even the war.

"You dirty rat!" cried Sydney, stealing a Cagney line as he hauled off and sent freckled-faced Spencer sprawling across the floor. A chair flew through the air, catching Wayne right square on the skull, but it didn't knock off his Stetson. As I lay there dazed a moment, I had the feeling the noise they were making was coming from somewhere else, or that it had been recorded a long time ago.

Determined to get out of there while I could still walk, I got up and headed toward the doors, where I was met by a chocolate cream pie right in the eye. Humphrey Bogart stood there in the flesh, or whatever, with a hostess cart loaded with pies, and he was slinging them—laughing and having one helluva time. Everyone who approached him got slammed with a strawberry shortcake or banana cream or coconut custard. The pie in the eye made me more angry than the fist in the ear. And I tried to get my hands on a lemon meringue, but got one in the chest instead. Ugh! By that time the cart was nearly empty, and all of us were gooey. Bogart had succeeded in stopping the fight.

In the auditorium downstairs it sounded like the snappy delivery of Jack Lemmon. "This clip of the love scene between Hoffman and Streisand will give you a good idea of why this film has received three nominations . . ."

One by one we climbed out from under tables or behind chairs, peeled ourselves off the walls and floor, and scraped the slop off our faces and clothes. I was the only one breathing heavily.

"Now that everybody's a little more relaxed"— Bogart laughed cynically,—"I have an announcement to make."

Only then did I notice that Syd had the film tin notched in his white knuckles. "I have no time for speeches," he said, the mountain man moving toward the projection room.

"You *damn* fool," Clark said.'That's what I've been tryin' to tell you." He pointed at the film case. "That's not *Escape to Monte Carlo*."

Syd looked like a monkey with an empty peanut shell.

Edward G. demanded, "Look for yourself if you don't believe us."

"What you've got there is *Gidget Goes to the Beach.*" Tracy laughed bitterly.

Syd looked as if he'd been struck by lightning. "You mean to say—"

"That's right. The reporter duped all of us."

Everyone turned to stare at me, and no one seemed to notice that I was just as surprised.

"Ladies and gentlemen," said Bogey, "if you'll just shut your traps a minute, I'll be able to clear up your confusion. It so happens I have *Monte Carlo*."

Syd inquired, "You have the film here at the Plaza?"

"He hasn't got a thing," said Edward G. "He's just trying to upstage everybody, as usual."

"You can rattle your jaws all you want," Bogey said, "but I'm here to make a deal."

"If you do have it," Clark said, "dealing with Syd would only be cutting your own throat."

"That's what you think, Clarky boy. You better take a hike around the movie houses in Chicago and New York and L.A. sometime. Or just sit home and watch your TV. Who do you think you're gonna see spittin' in your eye? Heh! Heh! Heh!" Bogey laughed hoarsely again, and out of the puddle of his eye rose that terrifying gleam I'd only seen once before: when he'd gone mad in *The Treasure of Sierra Madre*.

"Don't be a dumb ass," said Wayne. "We're on TV too. But the public's fickle as a high-school cheerleader. One day they love you, next day they forget you."

"Not me, Trigger,"Bogart laughed. "Not with this face," and he tugged at the doughy substance of his cheek. "Not with this charm," and he batted his eyelashes.

"Some critic who wasn't even born when you were a hot ticket is going to come along and write you up as a rotten ham," said Spencer. "And the public will believe it. Every word. All of a sudden they'll stop showing your films. The plain truth is that you need this 'Black and White' syndication deal as much as anybody. Maybe even more."

"Keep your two cents to yourself."

"You're nothing but a fad," said Clark.

Bogart looked like he wanted to tangle with Gable, and I would've enjoyed watching two tough-guy film giants wrestle on the dusty floor like a couple of special-effects dinosaurs. But Humphrey looked around at the two gangs and thought better of it.

"If Syd's mob shows that film and gets the syndicators interested," said Gable, "they might end up cutting your film out of the package."

"Not a chance! If they cut anybody's film, it's going to be you and Colbert in that silly trifle by Capra."

"Think you got it all figured out, don't you?" snarled Edward G.

The doors swung open, and there stood Marilyn Monroe in a sleek red dress. She moved slowly as a tiger getting ready for a kill and pulled up beside Bogey. "They just won't accept that we don't need them," she said, looking at him and then at the rest of us. Her eyes came to rest on my face only a moment. Not even a blink of acknowledgment did she give me.

So that's how it was. Marilyn had switched the films at Goldwine's penthouse, and she had screwed everybody, including me. Just like I always knew she would.

Crawford peered at Monroe, Gable stared at Bogart, and Wayne muttered, "Outlaws!"

"So it's a partnership," said Syd. "Well, I'm a practical man. Mr. Gable can feed you all the philosophy he wishes. Personally, I am prepared to talk business. I will give you one million clams for the film."

I suspected he actually did mean clams rather than dollars. But I was hurt anyway: they'd offered me only twenty-five thousand.

"Where're you gonna get that kind of dough?" Edward spat.

"Unlike your ilk," said Syd, "our class of actor doesn't find it necessary to spend every farthing the moment it reaches our fingertips. We have invested wisely."

Tracy and Gable glanced at each other, and their worried looks made me think the membership dues in their gang weren't paid up, that they couldn't approach that offer. Too many stars had gone bankrupt keeping up the appearances of being a star, I guess, while the supporting actors of Hollywood could live in garden apartments and no one would think them the worse for it.

"One million smackers!" repeated Sydney. "That can purchase a lot of fedoras, Humphrey."

I was dizzy with all those zeroes.

"You guys really crack me up," said Bogey. "I want to make a deal, all right, but it's not money I'm after."

"Gold nuggets," said Gable snidely. "He never got over that movie."

"No, my slimy, talentless friend. It's power of another kind I'm interested in."

"You want us to crown you king?" Spencer Tracy sneered.

Bogey broke into a wicked, gurgling laugh, like a man dying with a joke on his mind. "Very astute of you, Dick Tracy. It's royalty I'm after, all right. Not king, but prince. I want . . ."—he hesitated—"I want to play . . . Hamlet."

"What!" we all cried.

"You heard me! All my life I wanted to play that role. But they teamed me up with fatso over there, and had me doing Hammett instead of Hamlet."

"You'll make a *great* Hamlet," Marilyn said to Bogey, patting his shoulder.

"Humphrey, for old time's sake," said Syd. "Time is running out for me. Any gain in my standing could help boost our film, *Casablanca*, as well."

"*Our* film. Don't flatter yourself, old boy. Anyway, you don't hear too good. I want someone to produce a full-fledged film of *Hamlet* with Humphrey Bogart in the title role."

Syd shifted gears quickly. "Why, yes, there are possibilities in the idea, of course. Two great artists—Bogart and Shakespeare—the result could be a great event."

"I thought you'd see it my way. But there's one catch. I want it to be released for a living audience, not for the likes of you and me."

Syd's jaw dropped, the only time I ever saw him lose his cool.

"You must be nuts," said Clark.

"It can't be done," sputtered Robinson.

Straightening his tie, Sydney Greenstreet stepped forward. "I for one am not prepared to make such a blanket statement. Let's talk to the experts."

"It's one thing to screen a film like *Monte Carlo* that's

already been shot," said Gable. "But you know damn well you can't make another film once you're only celluloid."

"The cameras couldn't even photograph us."

"I wouldn't be so sure about that," said El Syd. "The greatest cameraman of them all, Billy Bitzer, happens to be a resident of The Big House, and if anyone could do it, Billy could."

"Syd's trying to con you," Spencer said to Bogart.

Clark took two steps toward Bogey.

"Just keep your distance there, Clarky boy," said Humphrey. "I can hear you just fine right where you are."

"While it has always seemed reasonable to assume an absolute separation between one's life and one's image," said Sydney, "to my knowledge no one has ever actually challenged it."

Clark was distressed. "He's lying to you. It can't be done, and he knows it." His hands were fists at his sides. "He's playing up to your puffed-up head."

"We've already begun to refurbish The Big House on Long Island. The main studio could be cleaned up rather quickly. Platforms constructed. Sets built."

"How long do you figure it would take to get rolling?" Bogey asked.

Syd thought it over. "A maximum of three months."

"Three months!" said Gable. "Three years is more like it."

"Three months is too long," said Marilyn, hanging on to Bogey's arm.

"Damn right," said Bogey, "much too long."

"Of course, segments of the film could be shot outdoors on our spacious estate," said Syd. "Meanwhile, the carpenters could be working overtime in the studio. Interior scenes could be inserted later. Fact of the matter is we could start shooting almost immediately. That is, after you have finished studying the script."

Bogey pulled free from Marilyn's hold. "I've been studying it for years. I know *Hamlet* by heart! Ahem. 'O that this too sullied flesh would melt, thaw and resolve itself into a dew, or that the Everlasting had not fix'd His canon 'gainst self-slaughter—' "

"Oh, shut up!" said Robinson.

Greenstreet was obviously trying to keep his composure, though only too well aware of the progress of the Awards. "In that case," said Syd, "I could begin casting immediately—I know just the right person to play the fair Ophelia."

Marilyn took hold of Bogey's arm again.

"I personally approve all lead roles," said Bogey.

"Of course, of course."

"Who'd you have in mind?"

"Miss Lauren Bacall."

Bogey gasped, and Marilyn jumped. "Not that bitch! Bogey, don't forget what you promised me."

"Sure, baby, sure."

"*You* as Ophelia," said Tracy, shaking his head sadly at Marilyn.

"I've always wanted to go legit, and this could be my last chance."

"Any old horse thief can see that Syd's leading you on, Humphrey," drawled Wayne.

"Clam up, all of you," said Bogey. And then to Sydney, "Lauren's still in the flesh."

Marilyn's face suddenly looked old.

Sydney had now moved up beside Bogart, and said quietly, "There's no telling what we could accomplish with Billy Bitzer's genius behind us. Indeed, Miss Bacall is in attendance at the Awards, and we might well be able to effect a deal this very evening."

"Yeah," said Bogey, "who's to stop us?"

"I am!" said Marilyn, and she scooped the last cream pie off the cart and slung it at Bogey, who ducked aside. The pie hit John Wayne in the Silver Star.

Wayne's gun hand jerked to his side, but he wasn't wearing a holster.

"Take it easy, baby," groaned Bogey. "I haven't forgotten you. Just leave everything to me."

"Like hell! You're the same as every other man," said Marilyn, and she stalked out. I was tempted to run after her, to comfort her, but she had done me wrong.

"Well, sir, do we have a deal?" Syd pressed.

"You bet your sweet carnation we do," said Bogey, glancing toward the door that Marilyn had exited through.

"That's what you think," Gable sparked, rushing Bogey. In moments the Humph was surrounded by Edward G., Gable, and Tracy, and they started searching him in a very unfriendly way.

"Heh, heh, heh." Bogart coughed. "You guys give me the chills."

"You said it, buster," said Gable. "We're gonna keep you on ice 'till the show's over. Then, frankly, I don't give a damn what deal you make with Greenstreet."

This made Bogey laugh all the louder, puzzling not only Gable and his cohorts, but yours truly. "Heh, heh, heh, heh, heh—"Bogart couldn't control himself. Finally, he wiggled his finger toward a face in the small oval window in the dim projection room.

From the stage below we could hear the voice of Jimmy Stewart: "You're going to have an opportunity to see some of the most spectacular special effects ever captured on film. . . ." There was a low rush of human noises, and then we heard music swirling up out of the sound system. Not the sweeping computer-generated audio spiral of outer space, but tinny music: clarinets and cornets and violins, the kind of music that was a lot of sentimentality and little substance, the kind moviegoers were conditioned to react to with feelings of mystery and exoticism and romance forty years ago. Music that conjured up a blazing afternoon in Monte Carlo.

Bogey went on laughing.

$\triangledown$

16

RUNNING WILD

BELOW WE COULD HEAR the voice of Sydney Greenstreet rumbling out of the silver screen, persuading a dealer in fine gems to see things *his* way, or else.

The film droned on, and the audience got noisier. Then a woman's voice came over the microphone. "Is there a projectionist in the house? This is the Academy Awards of 1990, not 1936!" It sounded like Meryl Streep.

Wayne yanked on the door of the projection room again, pounded hard with his big knuckles, but Gable and Tracy didn't stir, overcome by the idea that the dice had stopped rolling and they had lost. Greenstreet, with a grin of immense relief smeared over his face, followed Bogart toward the swinging doors, discussing production details of "the greatest *Hamlet* the world would ever behold."

"Hey!" I shouted to Sydney. "What about my money?"

Sydney stopped short and pirouetted. Bogey looked too— so did they all. "Why, of course," said Greenstreet. "Drop by The Big House and I'll have a check waiting for you." And then the two of them disappeared out the door, and I could hear Sydney chirping happily over the fact that *Monte Carlo* seemed not to have been damaged by time's cruel assault.

I shouted after them, "I'm tired of getting screwed out of

what is mine!" They were gone even before I'd finished my short speech, and I realized that Crawford, Tracy, and Edward G. were looking at me like I was a . . ."dirty" . . .rat but they had bigger things to worry about than a misplaced person from the South Bronx. They shifted their eyes over to Gable, who had deep gashes of distress across his forehead.

Wayne said, "What're we gonna do now, boss?"

For a change, Gable's mouth wasn't making noise.

"We gonna just let 'em walk out like that?"

"Will you shut up and let me think?"

Wayne looked hurt.

"You've already done too much thinking," said Robinson.

"Pipe down!"

"We're whipped, and it's your fault. I just hope like hell it's your film that gets bumped from 'Black and White' and that you get the oblivion you deserve."

Gable's chest puffed up. "A lotta help you've been. Had to be dragged out here to save your own damn ego."

"You botched the whole deal, Gable. Now *we're* gonna pay for it."

"If you don't shut your face, I'm gonna put that cigar out in your ear."

"Someone's coming!" said Tracy.

Charlton Heston and Van Johnson pushed through the swinging doors. I skipped behind a partition, but the celluloid characters stood their ground, watching. Neither of the new arrivals seemed to notice any of the mess we'd made in our chair-breaking, pie-slinging brawl.

"I don't understand why the projectionists didn't answer the phone," said Johnson.

"Your guess is as good as mine," said Heston.

They went up to the door of the room, which had only one small oval window that was positioned too high to look into directly. Heston tried to twist the handle, but the door wouldn't open. Johnson started knocking.

The audience sounded like a crowd stuck in a stalled subway car, and the sound track seemed to get louder too. On the screen we could hear Linda Darnell mixing a shaker of cocktails for Greenstreet. "My deah lady, your assistance would be most invaluable," Sydney was saying, "and I am prepared to make it worth your while." On and off the screen he was promising to make things worthwhile.

"*If* I agree to go to Monte Carlo," said Darnell, "where would we meet?"

"At the Casino, naturally."

Outside the projection room Heston and Johnson were confused, frustrated, annoyed. "Open up in there!"

No response.

"Who was scheduled to work the projectors tonight?"

"Irv Hartack headed the team," Heston replied. "Been doing the Awards for years."

Johnson put his hear to the door, "Irv, are you okay?" Then, to Heston, "Maybe he's had a heart attack."

"What about the other projectionists? And why is that black-and-white film running? The door is locked from the inside. Something's wrong."

"Don't forget the projectionists recently agreed to a new contract," Johnson said. "Some dissidents still feel they're getting a raw deal."

"You think this is a union protest?"

Van Johnson shrugged and knocked hard. "Who's in there?"

"Open this door immediately," Heston said as if invoking one of the Ten Commandments.

When there was no answer, Heston rammed the door with

his husky shoulder. But the soundproof door was solid.

"Help me slide that table over here Van, so I can take a look inside."

Once the table was in place, Heston climbed up and peered through the little window.

"What do you see, Charley?"

"I'll be damned."

"What is it?"

"There's no one in there at all."

"We'd better have Security break in," said Johnson.

"I'll get Jack to settle down the audience," said Heston, jumping down to prove he still had spring in his legs.

After Heston and Johnson had marched through the swinging doors, Gable said, "The only thing we can do is get our tails downstairs and stop Syd from squeezing even more out of this mess."

"What's the use?" Robinson sighed.

"The public still has to react to the film, and the newspapers and networks still have to report what happened, and the syndicators still have to pick it up. None of this has happened yet. And maybe it won't happen if we can stop them from grabbing too much publicity."

"Now I've heard everything," said Eddie G. But there was a flicker in his dark eyes that seemed to say the idea made sense to him.

Now that he had some kind of action to take, Gable stepped with a bit of the old swagger toward the swinging doors. The rest of them stood there looking at each other a moment or two. Finally, all of them, including Robinson, hurried toward the doors.

"What about me?" I said, but they didn't even turn to look.

While I stood there in a stupor, wondering what was left for me—no money, no girl, no film, no job, no ticket back home, not even a pillow to rest my head on after 11A.M. the next day—I heard the door of the booth unlock. Instinctively, I stepped behind the partition again. Out of the door came Charlie Chaplin. Now he was dressed in his traditional derby, his threadbare, unpressed black suit, and those curious curled-up shoes. After looking around at the mess and seeing no one, he wobbled past the dessert cart and out the swinging doors.

As the film continued to reel, the audience grew more uneasy, their laughter becoming nervous, accented with an occasional Bronx cheer or shout of annoyance.

"Ladies and gentlemen," Jack Lemmon appealed, "it is important that you all remain in your seats. Someone in the projection room apparently has become ill, and Charlton Heston and Van Johnson are assisting up there right now. Everything will be back to normal presently. In the meantime, please remain seated. . . .For those of you watching the Academy Awards on your television screens at home, we apologize for this delay. But I'm sure you won't want to miss the exciting revelations in those little white envelopes, so please bear with us a while longer. Doc Severinson's orchestra will now . . ."

Into the projection room I moved cautiously, and when I saw no one else inside, I pulled off the overalls so I could move around better in my jacket and trousers. Then I snapped off the projector. The film groaned and stopped, and the audience hushed up, followed quickly by more buzzing. It took me a while to rewind the film, and my fingers felt rubbery as I removed it from the guide device. But I finally stuffed the reel into the film case, snapped the lid tight, and forced it into my trousers. Cold!

I headed for a fire-escape door I had seen earlier toward the far end of the building. By now there was a tremendous commotion down in the auditorium. Jack Lemmon had lost his cool the way he'd done in *The Out of Towners* and was shouting into the microphone, "Return to your seats! Do you hear me—sit down! Everyone sit down and stop behaving like a pack of animals!" At the fire door I pushed the long metal handle, but it didn't budge—the place was a firetrap. I was forced to head down the stairs, which I did in leaps. Luckily, I didn't run into anyone as I came out behind the backdrops of the stage.

There was a roar coming from the audience. Looking out through the curtains, I saw what looked like a scene out of *Phantom of the Opera*. A few thousand people were shrieking as they swarmed up the aisles like drunks on Times Square on New Year's Eve. Some were standing on seats shouting, and several were throwing punches at each other, and women in dresses were tripping and falling. Several had fainted. I spotted Wayne and Tracy pushing their way toward the stage, and I realized why people were panicking. They were being pushed and bumped around by unseen hands and bodies.

It was Wayne who spotted me, and I pulled back behind the curtain and moved along the wall. When I came to a power box, I started pulling levers. The house lights went out and a circle of strobe lights above the stage started flickering and flashing and a purple spotlight swung back and forth, creating a crisscross of Technicolor: it was like doing LSD with a hangover.

Just then I spotted the short round figure of Goldwine, checkered by the strobes, behind the backdrop. Apparently, they had patched him up pretty good, though he did seem a bit concave in the chest. Just what I needed—another spook on my trail. But I'd sort of been expecting him, sooner or later. With twenty million bucks in the bank, he should be able to bribe old man Death to get another walk-on part. To complicate things, the film popped out of my belt, and Goldwine turned his head and saw me trying to stuff it back into my trousers.

Ducking behind the curtains, I came to another fire exit. This time the emergency bar responded to my pressure, and just like that I was on a platform outside the building a dozen feet above the crowd of waiting fans. I ran down the metal stairs. Cold white beams were sweeping over the mayhem, and people were screaming and sirens were wailing. I kept running as fast as George Raft, breaking out of the stir.

I'm not sure how I got there, but an hour or so later I staggered into The Gold Rush. The film was still in my trousers, and the clerk was still at his post, staring at a talk show on the small portable TV. Merv Griffin was cozying up to one of the latest crop of starlets from a prime-time soap opera. The clerk's eyes didn't even buzz me as I passed the fake knotty-pine counter and slipped down the corridor. Unlocking the door, I dragged my body inside as if it were an overpacked duffle bag. I wouldn't have been surprised to find someone waiting for me. But only the hula dancers in the decals were occupying the joint.

Now that the madness of the night was only a buzzing in my head, and now that my trembling had stopped, a great depression poured into my chest like a ton of coal. I got out of my wrinkled clothes and dropped onto the sandy sheets and stared at the doorknob: it reminded me of my old pal Ferdy's face. Then I began playing Twenty Questions with myself. Wouldn't the syndicators be willing to talk big bucks with me now that I had the film? Not necessarily. Wouldn't both gangs be out to get me now? Most definitely. Wouldn't I have been better off leaving the film on the projector instead of bringing it with me to attract danger? Obviously yes. Wouldn't I be safer back in little old dangerous New York? Apparently so. Wasn't I a first-class jerk? Quite distinctly.

The self-hate made me feel a little better. I got up and clicked on the chubby TV chained to the wall. There it was all over again. The late news had its big story for the night—for the year—and the cameras had so much to catch that they didn't seem to know where to pan. People were fighting and falling and fleeing and maybe even fucking in that mass madness. I didn't catch sight of myself in the mob, but the pictures looked authentic, making it seem as though it all really had happened. At least the television seemed to think so. But the commentator was describing the scene with a breathlessness that made me feel queasy. Probably just hungry, I thought. I shut off the contraption, stashed the film between the mattress and box spring, and went out, making sure the door was locked behind me.

The heavy-lidded clerk was still staring at the TV. "You checkin' out?" he said, gazing at Griffin who was patting Brooke Shields on the bare arm.

"Just gonna grab a bit to eat."

His oily eyes aimed at me. "Maybe I could arrange a little entertainment when you get back?"

"A little entertainment—oh, you mean girls."

"Yeah, I mean girls."

I stood there gazing at the bare-breasted hula dancer on the wall over his shoulder, and said, "No, that's okay. I had my entertainment for the night—went to the movies."

"Suit yourself," he said, looking at me as if I were a cheap creep.

As I walked out, I wondered why I'd refused. True, I didn't have much money in my pocket, but that had never stopped me from buying something I really wanted. Maybe I was finally losing my taste for women, and I could live in peace.

On the street, thinly decorated with people—everybody must have stayed home to watch the Awards—I found my way to a grocery and bought a chilled quart of Coors, then stopped at McDonald's and ordered a large envelope of fries, plus a Big Mac served in its own Styrofoam coffin. After leaving I sensed there was something wrong with the place, but I couldn't figure out what it was. Then I realized that the McDonald's sign wasn't red and yellow, as it was everywhere else in the world, but a kind of gray with sepia letters. Maybe it was the night lighting in L.A., but I noticed, too, that other things seemed to be losing their color. To get a handle on reality I picked up the late edition of the *Los Angeles Gazette*. Already splashed across page one was the headline, "Riot at Academy Awards." So it really *had* happened.

It got into my head that maybe the clerk might check out my room and see what he could pick up as a tip. I headed back to the motel. By now I wasn't afraid of losing the film so much as being linked with the riot. People had gotten hurt, and there must've been plenty of property damage; there could be criminal charges. Sure enough, the clerk wasn't at his desk; the TV was ranting like an evangelist. I went down the hall with long steps. As I got to my door, out of the room popped the clerk, though he didn't seem to be carrying anything.

"What's the big idea?"

"Just checking to see if you swiped the towels."

"I told you I was coming back."

"That's what they all say."

When he left, I checked under the mattress: the film was still there. I dropped down on the dough bed, took my dinner out of the paper bag, and set it on the night table. Then I stuffed a cold stick of potato into my face and took a gulp from the beer bottle. Food out here just didn't have much taste, so I wiped my hands on the bedspread and picked up the newspaper to read all about it:

The riot began during the showing of an early feature film, *Escape to Monte Carlo*, featuring Sydney Greenstreet and Linda Darnell. The *Gazette* could find no record of this film in the filmography of the NGN studio. This has added fuel to the speculation that *Monte Carlo* may never have been officially released.

The questions that are even more puzzling, in the wake of the most devastating Awards evening in the history of Hollywood—in which three people were trampled to death and dozens were hospitalized—are these: Who screened the film? Why? And where is the film now?

Three people were killed! Did they mean *killed dead*? Or did they mean *movie killed*? I scanned the *Gazette* again, and crumpled the front page just to hear it. Finally, I lay back and closed my eyes. Suddenly it hit me that I was a very valuable person again. If not to Nadler or Greenstreet or Gable or Vianet, then to the world at large. I sat up. Everything that had happened at the Awards had instantly pumped up the value of the film. The only trouble being that if I tried to peddle it to any of them, I'd get nailed either by the police or the ghosts.

Realizing there was no way I'd be able to fall asleep too fast, I clicked on the TV and found a movie that was grainy enough to be worth watching. It was Bette Davis and Henry Fonda in *Jezebel*, and I settled back and watched half an hour before drifting off into my own private movies: a go-go dancer with little red fringes sprinkled over her pretty crotch was shaking her way along the bar, and Igor Lopes sprang up and stuffed a thousand-dollar bill between her legs.

$\triangledown$

17
DEAL AND WHEEL

THE SOUNDS CAME TO me through a long wet tunnel, like a dripping faucet amplified ten thousand times. Someone was pounding on the door. I flopped over and sat up as slowly as a man who'd been drinking gin all night. My head hurt. It didn't seem fair to have a hangover without having gotten smashed.

"Yeah?" I grunted through the door.

"Front-desk clerk. I've got no record of this room being booked."

"I paid the night clerk."

"Open the door and show me your receipt."

"I was just getting into the shower."

"Sorry, I just rented out this room, and the guest wants to get unpacked right away."

I didn't have the energy to argue, or even to take a shower. "Okay, okay. Give me a minute to get dressed."

I pulled the soiled shirt over my back and forced yesterday's socks, still on my feet, into my shoes. I was losing control of the day-to-day business of living, and didn't seem to be able to do anything about it. If only I could get one decent break. Now I heard the door unlock from the outside, and in walked Goldwine. The heavyset man waved off the

149

clerk, who was stuffing a greenback into his pocket as he headed down the hall.

Goldwine closed the door, pulled out a cap pistol, and used it to push me back inside. If possible, he was uglier than Von Stroheim, with rubbery skin that hung loose all over his face. And there was a mole the size of a bullet hole in his forehead that I didn't remember seeing before.

"How'd you find me?"

"I put Philip Marlowe—that is to say, Dick Powell—on the case."

"What's the gun for?"

"I want my property returned to me."

I began laughing spontaneously, nervously. "That wasn't the film you're after—it was *Gidget Goes to the Beach*. I got screwed just like the rest of them by Bogey and Marilyn."

"In that case, you won't mind letting me have the film."

"Sure, but what do you need it for? It can't be the money."

"The film has a special place in my personal history, for it was the first one I produced under my own banner. Now hand it over, or else."

"Help yourself. It's in a trash can on Wilshire Boulevard."

Goldwine placed the nozzle against my belly button and said gently, "Cough it up, or I'm going to make you cough up your guts."

Obviously, he'd been dealing with movie toughs too long, but he looked terribly serious, so I slapped his hand away and jumped the old boy. As we rolled around on the dusty carpet, the gun got between us and went off with a muffled blast. I grabbed my side, but then Goldwine slumped forward and rolled facedown on the floor. He had taken a slug, not me.

I scrambled to my feet, dead certain they'd heard the shot down at the front desk. Quick as in an old-time movie, I slid the film tin out from under the mattress, and dropped it into the cloth sack, along with the *Gazette*. Opening the back window, I looked back a moment. Goldwine was gone! I jumped out and ran across the parking lot, over a patch of brown weeds and rubble, through the yard of a garden apartment that had no garden. The air was dense as cotton soaked with alcohol. I hit another street and followed it. Had I killed Goldwine? No; how the hell can you kill someone who's already dead? And don't you need a body to have a murder? Maybe he'd jumped up and gone into the bathroom to patch himself up. But I didn't believe that was the case. He'd disappeared too fast. Just what *had* happened to his body, or whatever it was, after the shot went off?

My hands were shaking as I came to a wider drag with shops on both sides. A few men in shorts strolled by. Women were hugging packages like babies, peering into windows at the silky cloth and shiny beads. It occurred to me I hadn't seen any real kids out here—I guess they'd stopped having babies in Los Angeles. Then I realized I hadn't seen many people who were particularly old, either. In the smoke shop on the corner I picked up a copy of the *Los Angeles Times*.

Dragging my body into a coffee shop, I plopped onto a chair and ordered a cup of brew. My hands were still shaking as I pulled the *Gazette* out of my sack and compared its report on the riots with the one in the *Times*. Strange. The *Gazette* had played it up as big as World War II, while the *Times* didn't even mention that three people had been killed.

The coffee tasted flat, but it washed away the dryness in my throat, so I signaled for another cup. That's when I heard the two young would-be starlets at the next table, a couple of exports from Brooklyn, talking about the Awards blast.

"And I was gonna go down dere last night," said the brunette.

"Oh, you say dat every year," said the blonde.

"Really, I was all set to go."

"Well, good thing you din't—you coulda got trampled to death."

"Some weirdo took over the projector booth and ran this old-time flick."

"Why should dat start a riot?"

"How should I know? People started shovin' each other and fights broke out—it was like everybody'd gone nuts at the same secunt."

"What film was it?"

"*Monte Carlo* somethin' or other. And now it's missin'."

"Yeah, I heard on the radio some guy offered a quarter of a million bucks for the film. This private collector."

The hairs on the back of my neck stood up and took a bow. I flipped through the *Times* but couldn't find any mention of a reward. Leaning over toward the table of the two Brooklynites, I said, "Who'd be crazy enough to make an offer like that?"

"I beg your pardon?" The blonde suddenly moved from Bensonhurst to Park Avenue.

"Overheard you talking about the riot last night."

"You got a problem, mister?"

They thought I was putting the make on them, and in another time and place they might've been right. Either one would've made a pleasant one-shot connection. "Just wondered who offered the reward."

The blonde looked at the brunette and said, "Come on, Bambi, let's sit where we can have some *privacy*."

"Okay, Doris."

I felt like shouting, "You can keep your little maidenheads, only the frail membranes on those two hadn't made it out of grammar school. But at least they had given me a tip on a possible way out of my predicament. I paid up and left.

Outside, a wave of paranoia swept over me as I convinced myself the police were looking for me, and I berated myself for attracting unnecessary attention in the coffee shop. If people had actually died in that mess at the Awards, I could be in deep trouble. I didn't really cause the riot, but I certainly complicated the confusion by taking the film and flipping the light switches. And who would believe all that business about Monroe and company? No doubt Gable and Greenstreet were stalking the streets too, looking for me. Maybe even Bogey and Chaplin had joined in the search. And then there was Goldwine to consider. Probably he was up and about already, trying to return the compliment I'd paid him.

Everybody and his cousin were after me, and I had ten bucks to my name and no place to sleep it off for the night. Along the streets I went, thinking about all that money— two hundred and fifty thou for the coil of celluloid that I was carrying on my person. A quarter of a mil! But who had made the offer? Then I got the idea of calling the *Gazette*. At the edge of a small park I found a pay phone and got the number from information.

"City editor."

The operator connected me, and a tight-lipped secretary came on. I repeated myself.

"Who's calling?"

"A friend."

"May I say who's calling, *please*?"

"No, you can't"

"Sor-ry, he's on deadline now."

"Don't hang up! Tell him it's about what happened at the Century Plaza last night. Tell him it's about the missing film."

She smothered the mouthpiece with her hand, but I heard her. "It's another one." In a few moments the editor got on the horn.

"Yes, this is Brian Dunsworth." His voice was thick with annoyance. "Who am I speaking to?"

"My name doesn't matter, Mr. Dunsworth."

"It does if you want to continue this conversation."

"They call me Lejak, Eddie Lejak." As soon as I said that name I bit my lip—I was dropping clues all across the country.

"Okay, Mr. Lejak," he said with disbelief. "What can I do for you?"

"I'd like to make contact with the gentleman who offered the reward for the film."

"You and a hundred other jokers."

I wasn't tickled by his tone. "I've got a helluva good story here, and I can just as well call the *Times*. If you want first crack at it, let me know now."

"Go ahead and call the *Times*." He laughed, but he stopped abruptly. Reporter's grease was in his joints. Even with all the other false leads, he couldn't resist the possibility that I might be telling the truth. "What've you got?"

"The film."

"You know where it is and who's got it?"

"No, I mean I've got it."

A pause. "How'd you get it?"

"I was the one who shut off the projector last night."

"You were the projectionist?"

"I didn't say that."

An even longer pause. "You have the film with you?"

"I'm offering you a lead story in exchange for information—Gazette Recovers Flick That Doomed Three."

"That's a pretty fair headline—you a newspaper man?"

"Look, you get the story, and I get the dough. Want the deal or don't you?"

"Bring the film over right now. Ask for me. If you're not hear in half an hour, I'll write you off as another screwball."

"No deal. We've got to do it my way."

"What're you nervous about? Are the police after you?"

"My way or not at all."

Like other editors I've known and despised, this one enjoyed a buildup. "Let's hear it," he said.

"Okay. But tell your money man that if the police are tipped off, I put a match to the film."

"I got it. You want to take the money and run."

18

CELLULOID CONNECTION

THE SUN GOT TIRED of pumping light and dunked into the thick haze that lay over the city like the cheap carpeting in The Gold Rush Motel. It was almost time. After sitting on a bench in the four-block square park for about fifteen minutes, and making sure no one was near, I got up, strolled past the water fountain nonchalantly, then started pushing the garbage aside in a trash can. When I got halfway down, I pulled the film case out of my sack, laid it flat, and dropped my copies of the *Gazette* and *Times* over it.

It was twenty to six when I entered the Hair House across the street. The other customer was almost finished, taking some talc on the neck. I sat with my back against the wall and checked out a few copies of *Newsweek*, but they were too old to carry the story, so I checked out the pictures of the newsmakers: The American prez was declaring that "peace is the priority of this Administration," while on another page his secretary of defense was announcing that America's stockpile of nuclear weapons had nearly reached the sky.

I wondered if a New York shrink would have said it was significant that I chose a barbershop to run out the clock; that it showed I wanted, deep down inside, to look better;

that it meant I was demonstrating life-positive behavior.
Maybe I was drawing back from the edge of this weird
celluloid world and would be returning to my own kind: Ferdy,
Judy, Monica. If so, it was all due to one thing—the prospect
of a little piece of the American dream in my pocket.

Climbing into the chair closest to the window, I placed
my order: "Just a shave."

"How's about our special designer's shave?"

"No, thanks. Just one of your old-fashioned throat-rakers,
okay?"

The man, who had transparent skin and thick spectacles,
looked disappointed, but he rummaged around in a narrow
drawer under the mirror and came up with a straight razor.
Then he began strapping his blade sharp, just like they did
on First Avenue. "Wasn't that something at the Awards last
night?" he said. "Did you see it on TV?"

"Guess everybody in the world did."

As he smeared the hot lather on my face, I felt a chill
wriggle down my back. Then he began to scrape the blade
along my neck.

"Stars in gowns and tuxedos slugging each other—what
a sight."

"Yeah, real cute. Maybe you should write a script and send
it to the networks as a miniseries."

He looked at me kind of funny. "Say, that accent—you
from back east?"

"Me, no. I'm from Montana."

"Montana?"

"Easy on the sideburns!"

"Nice-looking hairpiece."

"It's just temporary. I had an accident and lost a patch."

"Want me to check it out for you?" There was a certain
morbidity in his tone, but I realized a change of appearance

might not hurt. "Sure, have yourself a fling." The barber undid the adhesive.

"Hair's coming back in fine."

The hairpiece had cost me a week's salary, but I didn't really need it. I knew it had only been an attempt to be someone other than Igor Lopes. I could see in the mirror that I didn't look much different with or without the piece.

A car pulled up near the phone booth across the street, and I flinched in the seat.

"Easy does it, friend. You want a shave or your throat cut?"

A man got out, tucked himself into the booth, started dialing. Then I realized it was a few minutes early; besides, the car was just a Chevy. Soon the man hung up the phone, got into his car, and drove away.

The barber finished right at six, but no other car rolled up. I wondered if something had gone wrong—or if they were setting me up. Maybe I shouldn't have given the *Gazette* editor so much info up front, I thought, getting edgy. With my contact not showing up by five after, I asked the barber to give me a trim.

At ten after six I asked him to snip the hair in my nose. By quarter after there was still no sign of my connection, and the barber was still trimming. If someone didn't arrive soon, I was going to be bald. If someone didn't come at all, I would be taking up residence in the park. I jumped out of the seat and gave him my last ten.

"What about your hairpiece?"

"That's your tip."

A sleek bronze Caddy slid up to the curb about fifty feet past the phone booth in the park as smooth as Ricky Henderson into second base. The driver popped out; he wore a dark uniform. Looking around, the man in the billed cap walked casually to the phone, tucked his head inside, and waited for the phone to ring.

It was now or never. Biting off a hangnail, I went into the drugstore, where there was a solitary pay phone, and reached into my pocket for change—all I had left in the world. Through the window I saw a huge gray truck pull up beside the trash basket in the park. A man in overalls got out, grabbed the trash basket, and shook the contents of it into the back of the truck.

Out the door I raced like a lunatic. "Hey, stop! You can't dump that trash!"

The garbage man climbed up into the cab of the truck and pulled away alongside the park. I ran to the phone booth, shouting and pointing at the truck, which had turned the corner.

"You must be Lejak," said the scrawny chauffeur, his face black and shiny as printer's ink.

"Yeah, and there goes the film!"

The two of us climbed into the front seat of the Caddy, and we drove away instantly. The excitement of money, money, money began to thud in my chest. Was it true? Was I really going to be a cash-carrying American pretty soon? If so, I'd be shopping for one of these battleships tomorrow morning. Only, I planned to have a bar and TV installed in the back. Plus a table, with a fresh rose in a crystal vase every day, and a folding bed. Then I heard this runny-nosed voice from the back: "What seems to be the problem?"

There in the middle of the wide seat sat this gimp of a thing, sunk so far down I hadn't even noticed it—or him. At least, I think it was a him. He had yellowish Shirley Temple coils drooping over his milky, creased forehead, milk-glass teeth, and jowls that flapped like a deflated balloon. The hand he hoisted to me was dead as a dog bone.

"If we don't catch up to that truck before the compactor mashes the film, we're all pissing in the wind."

Goldilock's eyes brightening, he screeched, "Did you see which way it went, Herman?"

"Yes, Mr. Robert."

So his name really was Friedlander Robert, and not the other way around. The wimp had a first name for a last name and a last name for a first name. No wonder he looked as if he had his ass on backwards. But if he wanted to throw his money around, I would be only too happy to take some off his hands.

Herman hit the gas and took a sharp right, but the truck was nowhere in sight. On closer look, the chauffeur might not have been black, after all, but could have been wearing blackface.

"You'd better not let him get away, Herman!"

I glanced at the package on the back seat, neatly wrapped in plain brown paper.

At the next corner Herman made another sweeping right turn, nearly clipping a young woman crossing the street, and Goldilocks screeched, "There it is! There's the truck!" He sounded like a brat who had just found his long-lost fire engine.

In less than a minute we passed the pachyderm of a vehicle. Then Herman swerved in front of it, forcing the driver to pounce on his brakes.

"Hey, you crazy son of a bitch!" the green-necked man at the wheel shouted at us.

I jumped out, and Herman got out his side.

"We think a baby was thrown out in the garbage," I said.

"What're you talking about?"

I pulled out my wallet, flipped it open to my all-purpose, fake ID card. "Official business. Open up the back." I pocketed the leather before he could get a good look at it.

The driver yanked on a lever in the cab to open the compactor lid, then got out and loped to the rear of the truck. Tons of the leftovers of Los Angeles were tightly packed in the bin, and I leaned over the iron lip and started prying the garbage loose with both hands—a sort of crazed prospector. The chauffeur rubbed his white gloves together, not about to get them soiled. Until Goldilocks cried out the car window, "Herman!" Then the chauffeur leaned forward without allowing his uniform to touch the truck and plucked a Campbell's soup can between two fingers. The stench of rotten garbage was powerful, but I located the film case and pulled it out. Slightly greasy, but it didn't seem dented.

"Herman," I said, jerking a thumb at the garbage man, "give the man a tip." And Herman did it! The garbageman stood with his jaw hanging loose, a twenty fluttering in his hand.

I tried to get into the back seat of the Caddy, but the door was locked. Goldilocks shook his finger at me and said, "No, no." So I climbed in the front again. The chauffeur got the engine humming and clicked the craft into gear. He wheeled right, and after a few minutes we stopped at the opposite side of the park. He kept the engine idling.

"My name is Friedlander Robert," said Goldilocks. "Who is Eddie Lejak?"

"Is this for *Who's Who in America*?"

"I'd just like to know how the film came into your possession."

"What for?"

"Collectors like to know the genesis of the objects they possess. It's a weakness of the beast." He giggled.

"If I told you that I'd have to up the price, so let's just get down to business."

"You stole it, didn't you?" Goldilocks seemed excited by the prospect.

"Do you want the film or don't you?" I said a bit too toughly, suddenly afraid he would nix the deal.

"Why else would I come to this part of town?" Goldilocks patted his curls.

"Well, you sure took your time getting here."

Goldilocks and Herman exchanged what mystery writers call a "meaningful glance," and the wimp in the back said, "May I inspect the film, please?"

Hesitating momentarily, wanting to see the money first, I decided to hand it over. Herman took it out of my hands, whipped the handkerchief out of his breast pocket, wiped off the tin, and then passed the film to his boss. I peeked at the package on the back seat again.

"Herman, hand me the torch."

The chauffeur reached into the glove compartment and pulled out a foot-long, golden flashlight, and passed it to Goldilocks, keeping an eye on me all the while.

I heard the tin being pried open, and the beam flashed over the satin ceiling of the vehicle. Suddenly I had another awful thought. What if the film had been switched at the motel when I'd caught the clerk in my room?

After a few tense, quiet moments, Goldilocks giggled. "You have a deal, Mr. Lejak." He handed the flashlight to Herman, and the brown package to me.

Once it was in my hands, I started breathing again. "You wouldn't be insulted if I checked it out, would you?" I said, already tearing into the corner of the heavy wrapping paper. "Not that I don't trust you, but I've waited a long time for this."

"Don't worry," Goldilocks said cheerily, "it's all there." He sounded as if he'd found someone to play jacks with.

Now I saw it—the greenbacks, the moola, the McCoy, the bread, the dough, the cash, the wherewithal—wads of the stuff that makes the world go 'round. I lost my breath again as I flipped the edges of the thousand-dollar bills; I felt like lighting a cigar with one of them. Gently I placed the package in my cloth sack, amazed that such a small bundle of wood pulp with a little green ink could promise so much pleasure.

The garbage truck plowed into the back of the Caddy. Goldilocks and Herman and I rattled around in the inner sanctum like marbles in a tin can. It must've dawned on the Captain of Sanitation that he'd been carting a treasure of one kind or another. And whatever went into his truck was his domain, so now he wanted a piece of the pie. The truck driver got down and headed toward the Caddy, and I got out the opposite side with my sack of moola.

While the professional drivers were calling each other names, I stumbled around the back of the truck and climbed up into its cab. Fooling around with the stick shift, I managed to back the beast into the street and take off. But it didn't exactly peel rubber. The driver easily caught up on foot and jumped up on the running board. Reaching through the window, he grabbed me by the throat, but I jabbed my fingers in his eyes and swung open the door. Off he went onto the street like a lump of putty.

Bumping along in the truck, I turned down one block after another, finally pulling onto a wide route. Though I kept expecting to see someone tailing me in the rearview mirror, I seemed to be on my own. Was it possible I was finally getting a few good bounces? I kept a steady foot on the pedal, looking for a sign indicating Los Angeles International Airport.

I wondered what had become of Sydney and Clark and Bogey. Not to mention Marilyn, especially Marilyn. After all, now we had a lot more in common—we'd both gunned down Goldwine. Though I had known from the start that so much beauty, so much sexiness could never belong to a guy with a name and track record like mine, I still couldn't get her out of my mind, I still couldn't help wanting her.

At an exit indicating Sunset Boulevard, I pulled off the highway. It took a while—I was fuzzy about directions and I wasn't driving a Ferrari—but I found my way to Goldwine's neighborhood, strictly upper crust. At last I rolled up behind the luxury apartment house where his penthouse overlooked the city. I had a hunch I would find Marilyn there, and I wanted to take one last shot at the whole stakes—the headlines, the money, *and* the girl.

I parked the heap near the service entrance, slipped inside, and took the stairs to the second floor before punching the elevator button. A man in a pale-blue suit was in it, but he didn't seem to be offended by me—probably thought I was a janitor. He got out on the tenth. On the fifteenth floor I got out, entered the stairwell again, and walked up to the penthouse through the dismal light. Even the best of joints had lousy stairwells. I stuck my neck slowly out the door into the corridor, making sure it was clear. Then I sank into the blue carpet and made my way toward the brass-handled double doors at the end of the corridor.

Suddenly I got nervous I might run into Goldwine. I wasn't sure of the proper etiquette toward someone you had wiped out. I leaned my ear against the white lacquered door. For a long while there was no sound at all. Then I heard something. Someone was sobbing. Marilyn! Though I didn't know if Goldwine was with her, I tried the door handle—locked. Getting too brave for my health, I knocked. No answer. I knocked again, loudly, then listened. The sobbing had stopped. Maybe Goldwine was taking revenge on her.

"Marilyn," I cried. "It's me. It's Iggy. Are you all right?"

In a few moments the door opened slightly. She was

wearing a white blouse and a black skirt, as if attending a funeral. When she saw me she opened wider and I squeezed inside. No one else seemed to be in the land of cushions and crystal, where we had gotten physical the day before.

"What's the matter?" I said.

To my surprise, she wrapped her arms around me tightly and pressed her eyes into my neck. I felt the wetness on my skin. While reminding myself that she and Bogey had done a number on me, I held on to her just as tightly.

"So Bogey gave you the business too."

All my snide comment did was make her sob again. And as I stood there peering over her shoulder toward the painting of the orgy on the floor, I saw a small shiny object on one of the cushions. Untangling myself from her arms, I went over and picked it up—her .32 automatic.

Marilyn looked at the gun and sobbed again.

People in Hollywood were getting so jaded that even one suicide wasn't enough for them. I slid the gun into my trouser pocket. "I'm leaving L.A." I said. "Maybe even the country. Would you consider . . . coming with me?"

Marilyn flickered through her tears and said, "Yes, Iggy, let's go far, far away and never come back."

"How do you feel about Monte Carlo?"

$\triangledown$

19
MONTE CARLO OR BUST

A JET-POWERED CIGAR CLIMBED into the wild black yonder.
The silence that followed was impressive too, nicked only by
the tick-tick-ticking of the roadster's engine cooling in the
airport parking lot.

"I'm glad you came to the penthouse when you did."

"Me too," I said, still unconvinced that someone in her
condition could harm herself.

"I guess it's true," she said, "I guess I really am a dumb
blonde. Even though I know I'm being lied to, I believe them.
A first-class sucker."

"You've got the same disease as this guy Ferdy in New
York."

Another jetliner screwed into the sky, and I noticed a strand
of blonde hair on my sleeve—actually it was Goldwine's sleeve.
The jacket I'd borrowed from his closet was baggy, dusty on
the shoulders, but very well made. I inspected the long, thin
piece of hair closely, and it seemed to be real.

"Before we go into the terminal, I'd like to know what the
deal was between you and Bogey."

Marilyn looked at me squarely and said, "The reason Bogey
and I got together is that both of us had a burning passion—"

"Just as I thought!"

"Hush, Iggy, and listen to me. We had a passion to change
our images."

"What's wrong with your image?"

"He's tired of being a tough guy, and I'm tired of being a
dumb blonde."

"Where does Chaplin fit in?"

"Chaplin had always wanted to break out of the slapstick
rut, so Bogey offered him the part of Laertes if he would help
us."

Her story was beginning to make sense, and this worried
me. I was also worried that she and Bogart were going to fake
me out again. "It was more than a business arrangement. I
saw the way Bogey was looking at you."

"No matter who Bogey looks at, he only sees himself.
Anyway, I never thought much of him as a romantic lead.
Now you, that's a different story—you turn me on."

"Me?"

"I could shack up with you from now 'til doomsday."

I knew I shouldn't tell her, but I couldn't help myself. "To
tell you the truth, Marilyn, I've been . . . in love with you
ever since *All About Eve*."

"I was a kid then."

"That's the girl I fell in love with."

"You loved Norma Jean?" She pointed her red-rimmed
eyes at me, then set her forehead in the crook of my neck.
But I placed my finger under her chin and raised the face
that had thrilled millions, the face that life had worked over
too hard; our mouths came together. Her lips were soft, and
warm, and salty. Didn't that mean they were not dead but
full of life, full of passion?

Marilyn flashed a fleshy thigh as she climbed out of the
roadster. I followed her into the terminal, convinced by every

shake of her hips that there was a God in heaven. Over the polished floor we slid to the Air France ticket counter, where I learned there was a flight to Monte Carlo, via Paris, within the hour.

Two one-ways," I said in distinct Bronx tongue to the Mexican clerk, who looked as if he'd played an extra in *Viva Zapata*. He stretched his neck uncomfortably at the noose of his orange tie. I thought he'd bug me about lack of reservations. But he immediately scooted off and began punching keys on a computer.

"You only need one ticket," Marilyn said.

I suddenly felt faintly nauseous. "I knew it! I knew you were going to ditch me at the last minute."

"I haven't changed my mind. I just don't need a ticket."

Cautiously relieved, I turned and said to the clerk's back, "Sorry, make that one ticket."

The Mexican seemed utterly unflapped by the change, as if he'd intended to give me one anyway. Kneeling down, I unzipped the cloth sack and slipped a thousand-dollar bill off the stack. Marilyn's eyes twinkled at the sight. But the clerk didn't even blink at the crisp bill with the three zeroes, turning to the electronic cash register. At last he handed over the ticket packet. Plus change, which I stuffed in the sack. It was great knowing there was more, plenty more where that came from, but I was suspicious about the clerk not checking out the bill. These days they were checking quarters for counterfeits.

In the terminal magazine shop I looked for a copy of the *Gazette* to see how the editor had played up the news tip I gave him. But the *Gazettes* were all gone. So I grabbed a copy of the late *Times* and went to sit out on a bench. I couldn't find anything on the first few pages about the exchange of the film for the dough.

"What're you looking for?"

"About last night. About the connection with Friedlander Robert."

"So it *was* you who grabbed the reel off the projector."

I didn't want to get into all that, not yet, so I just shrugged.

"You won't find anything about the exchange in the *Times*," she said. "It didn't involve the living."

What the hell does that make me? I wondered, and what about all the others? Did that mean Friedlander and Herman and the women in the coffee shop and the garbageman were dead too? That couldn't be. For one thing, I'd spoken at length to a newspaper editor about Robert's offer. When I pointed this out to Marilyn, she said, "He must've been with the *Gazette*."

"So what?"

"That's our paper."

I thought: God, could you please explain all this to me?

"Let me have the *Times*," she said. I handed it over, and she leafed through several pages. "Here it is."

I leaned against her as she read a small item on page thirty out loud: "'Friedlander Robert and his chauffeur, Herman Hills, were killed yesterday in a crash coming off the Freeway.

"Traveling in a Cadillac limousine, they were hit broadside by a garbage truck that went out of control and flipped over. The driver of the truck also died. . . .'"

"So that's why they were late."

"They were making the transition."

Folding the newspaper abruptly, I shook my head as if to rearrange all the information I'd been getting in order to understand it better. "If there's a separation between the two worlds, then how could Syd have hoped to stir up publicity among the living public?"

"*Escape to Monte Carlo* was made when he was still part of their world, so it can still have an effect on the living."

"Reading the accounts in the *Times* and the *Gazette*, I almost had the feeling there were two separate Academy Awards going on at the same place and time."

"There was only one event, but there were activities connected with the Awards that weren't available to both groups. Such as the fight outside the projection room."

"Yeah, such as the three people who were killed."

"One thing that was available to everyone was the film."

"But I saw the whole mess taped on television, just the way it happened."

"You saw it on our channel."

After letting this soak into my brain, I said, "So what's going to happen to Greenstreet and Gable and the rest of them now?"

"I don't think *Monte Carlo* screened long enough and the riot distracted attention from the film, so I doubt it will be picked up by the syndicators. But even if there were interest, Syd's gang would still have the problem of getting hold of the film, getting it to the syndicators, and somehow convincing them to take a chance on it. In other words, they're back where they started."

"What about the film Sydney promised to shoot with Bogey?"

"I think Sydney will have to keep his word—at least to try. Otherwise, Bogey will make trouble for him till the end of time. Besides, Syd would take a shot at it just to see if he could do the same for himself later on."

"Or maybe they'd have to be satisfied with showing the film to a much smaller market, to people like me, who can see all of you."

I guess she wasn't ready to talk about my condition, because she didn't reply. Suddenly I realized that a little old lady, in a black dress and black veiled hat, seated on the bench facing us, had been staring at me with wide eyes a long while, as if I'd been holding a conversation with myself.

In fifteen minutes we boarded the plane. Our seats were toward the back, and no one else took the third seat in our row. Nor did the stewardess try to be helpful. Soon a pair of men in trenchcoats, with the brims of their fedoras pulled low, sat down together a few rows in front of us.

"Uh-oh," I whispered. "Now what?"

"You're just overreacting."

"Are they like you or like me? I can't tell."

"Like me," she said, frowning in a way that made me feel self-conscious.

"They're obviously up to no good," I said.

"Probably involved in some other caper entirely."

"These things are going on all over the world, all the time? Under everybody's noses?"

"That's right."

It looked as though I wasn't going to be able to learn anything about my own condition by throwing hints at her. I was just going to have to come right out with it. "How come *I* can see you? How come *I* can hear you? How come *I* can . . . feel you?"

"It's because you're one of the walking dead."

Syd had made a comment to that effect at the Awards, though I'd thought he was just being grimly poetic. "Far as I've always heard, either you're dead or alive—one or the other."

"You've been living your life as if you were dead—doing nothing, feeling nothing, going nowhere, just not facing up to being human."

I'd noticed lately that the world had been turning black and white on me, but I couldn't help pointing out, "There's a lot of people like me around, 'specially in New York."

"And they all live with ghosts of one kind or another—the ones that are closest to them. Sometimes it's loved ones who are gone. Or people they want to love, or want to be like, but have little or no contact with. In your case I guess the actors and actresses you've been watching in the movies for years are the ones that mean the most to you."

"You mean to say that anyone connected with the movies—I mean I even saw old man Goldwine running around—is more important to me than my own Aunt Minnie? She died several years back, and I don't see her floating around."

"Kind of looks that way."

"But I had a run-in with a coupla chicks in a coffeeshop who knew about the reward, not to mention that garbage-truck driver who was killed in the accident."

"All of them must've had some important connection with the movies."

"Yeah, they're all probably writing scripts."

"Or else they live the movies in their minds, just like you."

Promising myself I would quit watching movies, I said, "I ought to tell you something else about Goldwine. He tracked me down at my motel, and he pulled a gun on me. There was a struggle, and the gun went off. Goldwine got hit, and then he sort of . . . disappeared."

"Beautiful!" said Marilyn. "Every chance I get I'm going to wipe him out."

It seemed pointless to go on killing the same person, but I guess that's the way it goes in the movies.

Without warning, Marilyn's expression turned serious, her faint eyebrows nearly meeting in the middle of her forehead. "Iggy, you can't stay in the middle anymore. Once this plane lands in Monte Carlo, there won't be any turning back. You'll be the same as me."

***

The jet engines were crooning like Bing Crosby. All of a sudden my head felt heavy and my body felt weak. I hated to make the kinds of decisions where it had to be left *or* right, up *or* down, right *or* wrong, good *or* bad—no in between, and no time to kick it around. I suppose that's why I tucked my head into the fuzzy crest of blonde hair just to my left, trying to escape once again. And because of all the crazy running around and excitement and tension, I actually did slip away right there on her shoulder.

I dreamed I was on a pure white strip of sand outside a huge casino, smoking a joint, watching the bikinis stretch by, when this immense black Packard pulled up on the beach and two thugs in trenchcoats and fedoras popped out and said they had been following me for years, and that they were going to teach me a lesson once and for all. I whipped out a chrome .32 automatic and fired twice and they went up in smoke, but after a while the back door of the Packard opened again and out came the same two thugs, and they introduced themselves as the ghosts of the ghosts I'd just rubbed out, and said they were going to teach me a lesson. I fired again, making them disappear, but they returned again and again, and I realized, there within the walls of my subconscious, that I would have to go on killing them 'til the end of time—that there would be no getting away from them.

The fat wheels of the plane chirped against the concrete, waking me up. I expected Marilyn to be gone. Yet there she was beside me, her brittle bleached hair in my face. I raised my head. "Guess I dozed off."

"Dozed off? You've been out for hours. We just landed in New York."

"Must've been a little tired," I said sheepishly.

"You've had quite a day," Marilyn remarked. I noticed the

skin of her neck was white as cocaine, and her hand seemed to have no weight on mine.

The voice of the pilot came over the intercom. "We'll be resting at Kennedy International Airport for twenty minutes. Next stop will be Orly Field in Paris, France. Then on to Monte Carlo."

"Iggy, this is your last chance," said Marilyn, her face glazed and expressionless, as if she didn't want to influence my decision.

I glanced out the round window. The sky was drawing a pallid freshness from the morning sun, polishing the bay into a hard metallic surface. Far beyond the water I saw a row of cars glinting in the low light, heading for Manhattan. In the island borough, the people were already neck-deep into this day. Fish were being dumped into big wooden bins, and cases of milk cartons were being delivered to school cafeterias and bagels, still warm, were being dropped off in brown paper bags at the neighborhood grocers. Vegetable stands were being replenished with tomatoes, and dogs were being walked and young couples were jogging through the park. Only the hookers could afford to sleep until noon.

If I stayed on the plane, and continued the trip, the money would be real and Marilyn would be mine. At least for a while. But the ultimate destination would not be Monte Carlo anymore; it would be some cavern deep inside my mind, out of which I would never find my way again.

When the pilot's voice over the speaker called for passengers to return to their seats and prepare to take off for Paris, I tightened up inside. Marilyn looked at me; neither of us moved. Finally she leaned over and pecked the corner of my mouth. "Iggy, you'd better hurry." I couldn't feel her lips, but I saw an opal gleam in each corner of her eyes.

I rose out of the seat and moved toward the front of the

plane, and though the lanky hostess looked as though she had a notion of intercepting me, she let me pass out of the plane and through the boarding tunnel. In moments I was in the Air France waiting area. I felt even more alone than I had in the lobby of the Century Plaza among all those stars.

Through the long windows came the sun, as brash as a New York kid, heating up the counters and seats and candy machines. In five or ten minutes they sealed up the door of the plane. As I stood watching out the window, unable to find Marilyn in any of the oval disks of glass, the jet began to roar. When the blast intensified, the silvery craft drew away from the loading dock and rolled out onto the runway. I kept staring as it built up momentum and took off into the air, became a shiny splinter, and disappeared in the clouds.

Only then did I turn away and move out into the main terminal, where the people were rushing and lugging suitcases and kissing good-bye. Several were crying. My cloth sack of money and Goldwine's jacket were still on the plane, so I went out into the world more or less the way I had come into it—empty-handed.

$\triangledown$

20
THE JIG IS UP

My FEET, AS FAR as I could tell, weren't moving. Yet my body went forward straight and steady through the airline terminal, as if I were on one of the conveyor belts that transport the luggage. The curved spires of steel supporting the stone-gray panels of the spacious building added to my sense of flight.

Abruptly I found myself outside, grounded, and there was a yellow cab resting at the curb. I climbed in. "Take me to Manhattan."

"Why not? I got nothing better to do."

Not only was he a wise guy, but he drove too damn fast and cut off several cars on the way. Once he nearly got us killed—a bus missed us by inches. All of which made me jittery. It was just as well I wasn't going to pay him.

In the tunnel we got caught in the grind of commercial traffic, the fumes thickened and there beneath the river I could feel a growing pressure in my chest. At last we rolled out of the Midtown Tunnel, and New York came busting back into my consciousness as we bumped in and out of the potholes up First Avenue. I saw a drug transaction being conducted on a streetcorner while a policeman stood on the opposite side lecturing an old man who had crossed against a "Don't Walk" signal. Farther up the avenue, two men stood in the gutter shouting angrily at each other over who had found a parking meter first. On another corner a mother slapped her small daughter so hard the kid fell onto the sidewalk. New York does terrible things to human beings, I thought.

Maybe all I needed was to move to another city, or some small midwestern town, and start a new life. Maybe work in a hardware store or learn to be a carpenter. But as we swerved— just barely missed running down a stray dog—I admitted that wasn't my problem. What I needed was something to believe in. The few times I'd been dragged to church as a kid had apparently made some impression on me, because whenever I got into a serious jam I thought about God. But it was only because I wanted protection. It wasn't real belief. What did I believe in, then? Thinking this over a few moments, I figured that I must believe in life; otherwise, I would've stayed on the plane.

When we finally pulled up in front of my tenement, I said, "Look, friend. I don't have any money," and got out of the cab.

The cabbie sprang out and met me on the sidewalk. "Let me get this straight. You had me drive you all the way from Kennedy to this crummy neighborhood knowing you had no money to pay for the ride?"

"I've got a television in my apartment, and you can have it. Okay?"

The cabbie, who was short and husky enough to have no neck, clutched my sleeve as he thought this over. "What size is it?"

"Well, it's thirteen inches, but it plays real good. For a black-and-white set."

I didn't even see them coming, but I felt the force of his knuckles lift me off the ground. Next thing I knew I was sitting on the concrete, the left side of my face throbbing. A kid in green sneakers walked by pointing and laughing at me. At least the cab was gone, and I'd paid up . . . in the oldest currency known to mankind.

Standing up, holding my sore cheekbone, and looking over the building where I sort of resided, I couldn't avoid certain conclusions—it was ugly, broken down, still standing only because there wasn't anyone willing to lay out the cash to knock it down. And it was only because I had spilled some beer there, and had a few pairs of socks in cold storage there, that I was returning to it.

Up the stone stairs—someone had written "fuck you" in chalk on every step—I went. As I was passing the door of the superintendent's rooms, I realized the rent was due again. Nor had I caught up with the two previous months. I stepped quietly up the wooden stairs.

At my door I remembered the money I owed Ferdy, and I wondered about my job. Sharpening these realities was the room itself, with everything dumped all over the floor; either the gangs had returned or some bag people had discovered the door unlocked and had set up housekeeping for a while. Well, at least no one was here now. Just me and the roaches. And I would try not to get in their way. I shut the door gently, without even allowing the latch to click, and sat down on the side of the mattress.

After a few minutes without any thought passing through my brain, I had a notion to call Ferdy. Lucky for him my phone was dead. The computers at New York Telephone must finally have tracked down my overdue bills. Lying back, I closed my eyes, but I was afraid I might fall asleep—I might dream! Hungry for the first time in days, I got up and checked out the dented refrigerator, and came up with a hard, curled slice of American cheese and a shriveled apple that looked like a shrunken head. Not too appetizing, especially since the apple reminded me of Eddie Lejak.

Maybe Lejak had calmed down by now. I wondered what day of the week it was. No matter. Even if it were Saturday or Sunday, Lejak would be at the office, writing headlines or repasting layouts. It was worth a call, if I could find a phone with a dial tone. I went downstairs as quietly as I'd gone up, and out onto the street. On the corner was a pay phone, but some junkie had torn out the coin box.

Two blocks away I found a phone with a hum in it and I fed it a quarter. All I had left was two dimes, two nickles, two pennies.

Monica picked up, so it had to be a weekday. "*Squealer.*"

"Hi, sweetheart, it's Igor."

"Where you been?" she said distractedly, as if doing her nails as she spoke.

"Just got back from Hollywood."

"Yeah, and I jetted in from Miami."

I was tempted to defend my statement, but I asked for Lejak instead. "Don't tell him it's me. I want to surprise him."

"He'll be surprised, all right."

I heard a click, and then the rushed tone of Lejak, "Hello! Hello? Anyone on this line?"

"Hello, Eddie. This is Igor." The moment he heard my name, he hung up. It wasn't the first time he'd done that to me, and I'd still managed to talk my way back into a job. So I began walking downtown, in the general direction of the *Squealer's* office.

I passed a movie house where they were showing a new one with Jack Nicholson, and I felt a strong urge to sit in the dark and stare at the screen. But it was too early for the theater to open, plus I didn't have the price of admission.

Anyway, movie screens were getting so small it almost wasn't worth going anymore.

By the time I reached the *Squealer*'s building, I'd decided not to take on Lejak without a little help. I pushed through the revolving door, moved across the dim, gray interior of the lobby to the pay phone, and dropped my last coins—thirty-two cents—into the slot. I gave AT&T every penny I had to achieve a kind of poetic purity in being totally broke. I dialed 373-2133, a number burned into my mind for the rest of my life.

"*Squealer*."

"Monica, let me have Ferdy."

"Oh, it's you again." Now she was chewing a wad of gum. Another click, and then I heard Ferdy's voice: "Copy desk."

"It's Igor."

"Didn't you go to Hollywood?"

"I went; now I'm back."

"That was fast."

"Listen, I'm down in the lobby. Could you come down a minute?"

"Don't tell me you need more money—I'm broke."

"No, no, Ferdy, honest. Just want to see you a minute."

A pause, then: "Okay. Be right down."

In a few minutes the automatic elevator doors slid open and produced three people, one of them Ferdy. He was wearing another pair of those bargain-basement slacks and had both hands in his pockets, as if holding tightly on to any money he had.

"What's up?"

"Look, I called Lejak earlier to see if I could talk to him about getting my job back, but he hung up on me. Any chance you could talk to him for me?"

"Whenever your name is mentioned, he goes right off the ledge. I'll just end up losing my job too."

"You know, Ferdy, if you don't help me get this job back, I'm not gonna be able to pay you back."

Suddenly Ferdy's face turned dark red, and I really thought he was going to take a poke at me. "You son of a bitch!" He turned on his heel and stumped back to the elevator.

The elevator hadn't shown up, so I could've tried to talk to him more, but it was very hard to get Ferdy mad, so I knew it was for real. Besides, I felt bad about using that kind of trick on him and thought it would serve me right if I lost my only friend in the world.

Once again I was on the street, heading uptown, though for no particular reason. It was just a direction to go, so I went. I spent most of my walking time trying not to notice the garbage in the gutter, the car fumes I was taking into my lungs. When I reached Fifty-seventh, waiting for the stalled traffic to get moving, on an impulse I jerked my thumb toward the bridge that spanned the river. The guy who happened to be stopped there opened his window and said, "Hop in." Easiest hitch I'd come across in my life, so I got in.

The car, a green import the size of a lawn tractor, was fairly new, and the driver was young, which was good because those old-timers gab too much. Near as I could figure, he was the real McCoy. His nose was too crooked for an acting career, and he was as skinny as a baseball bat. From here on in, everybody and everything was going to be real.

"How far you going?"

"Far as you can take me."

I lay my head back and absorbed every bounce without a word. Every so often I looked out at the surroundings—the steel girders of Astoria that supported the subway tracks, the Greek and Italian delicatessens, the Spanish women pushing baby strollers. But I didn't learn anything I didn't already know about the world, so I shut my eyes. I must've dozed off, and I'm not sure for how long, but when I felt the car stop my eyes blinked open.

"What's up?" I inquired, twisting my neck toward the driver.

"Hand over your wallet," he said pleasantly, waving a dandy-looking red stiletto in my direction.

Sitting up, and shaking my head sadly, I said, "You might as well carve me up, 'cause I don't have a nickle to my name."

This news made him angry, and for a moment I thought he was going to slice me with the stiletto just because I was broke. "Get the hell out of my wheels."

Opening the door slowly, I climbed out, advised him to have a good day, and stood there on the desolate street facing a row of split-level houses. The car sped off, and I started walking. I kept on walking and walking, out past the houses and shopping malls, beyond the hydrants, along the edges of potato fields and among the maples. It reminded me of the way some character in a book I'd read a long time ago had walked into the sea and just kept walking until there was no sand left to walk on.

$\triangledown$

21
GATES OF HEAVEN

AN HOUR, A WEEK, or a year later a pair of tall iron gates loomed before me, unlocked and unattended. By now, the afternoon sky looked glazed like the inside of a seashell, and I felt light-headed from all that walking. I passed inside the gates and walked along the winding path, up the slope, through the bent birches and low hedgerows. At the edge of a pine grove I stopped, gazing up at the high, wide, concrete-faced building.

Slowly I moved toward the big-boxed structure, crunching over the marble chips. The salmon-colored Studebaker was parked out in front, and there wasn't a dent or a scorch on it. For some reason this seemed perfectly reasonable to me. Up the great staircase I moved. At the landing, I knocked on the mahogany door without much force, and I wondered if it could be heard within.

In moments the door unbolted, and there was Arthur Treacher, dressed up, as usual, like a penguin. "How do you do, sir," he said as if surprised to see me. "Have you been traveling long?"

"To long," I said. "I'm bushed."

"Please come right in," he said graciously, a tinge of superiority curling into the corner of his mouth. "I'll show you to the drawing room."

Treacher escorted me inside, and we moved down the long corridor in silence, past the statues and portraits and old-time projectors. A Flying Tiger fighter plane had been rolled in to beef up the collection. When we reached a pair of double doors, he slid them open, and there was Syd seated in a red leather armchair, chasing an olive around his martini glass. Licking his pinky, he looked up and declared, "Igor! I thought we had seen the last of you."

"So did I."

"Come in. Come in."

I went in.

"You know I ought to be angry with you," he said.

"Sorry if I caused you any grief, but for once I had to do something for myself." At this time I took Marilyn's pistol out of my trouser's pocket and aimed it at him.

"*Per*fectly understandable, my deah boy, but I do wish you'd put that gadget away. Weapons do not promote hospitality."

"My job is gone, and my room is overrun, and my phone is dead, so I came to get the money you promised me for my help in the fight at the Century Plaza."

"You're entitled to every penny, of course, but I have a proposition that may benefit you even more."

"I don't want any more con jobs. I just want what's coming to me."

"Why don't you sit down and hear me out."

"I don't want to sit. I just want my money."

"The money is yours, but I'd also like to offer you a job. The pay is good, and it comes with an apartment, rent-free, here at The Big House."

In spite of being wary, I was interested. "What kind of job?"

"We could use your writing skills to help adapt *Hamlet* for the screen."

"You're going ahead with it?"

"Your running off with my film forced me to take Humphrey Bogart's proposal much more seriously, and I began to see possibilities that had not occurred to me earlier."

"What're you talking about?"

"In short, I am going to play the role of Polonius."

El Syd looked genuinely pleased, not vengeful in the least.

"You're not out to get me for taking the film off the projector?"

"All's well that ends well. Now, please put away that gun."

Slowly my gun hand sank.

Sydney Greenstreet set his martini down, stood up, and said, "Come, I want to show you something."

I put the gun back in my pocket, but held on to it as I followed him out the doors. Syd went briskly—if that's the right word for someone his size—down the corridor. After a three-minute walk I began to hear the sounds of saws and hammers. "Right in here," he said, and we came out on a platform above the huge studio that Marilyn and I had cut through a lifetime ago. Looking out over the vast space, I saw dozens of men and women measuring and cutting and painting large sheets of canvas and wood and cardboard.

"The castle of the Prince of Denmark will be rising before your very eyes!" Sydney declared proudly.

I was impressed by the scope of the project as well as by Syd's obvious commitment to it. "It sounded to me as though you were giving Bogart a line about shooting the film. Now you look gung-ho."

"That is because I am much more confident of its ultimate success."

"What changed you mind?"

"Essentially two factors. One, we have called in Hans

Holzer, the noted supernaturalist, to work with Billy Bitzer, the great cameraman; they will conduct screen tests using a special motion-picture camera invented by Holzer that can capture essences on film. Two, we are already in contact with one of the walking dead, Brendan Foster, who is vice-president at a major distributor, and he has agreed to attempt to launch our *Hamlet* for a living public. Of course, there are major obstacles in this regard to overcome, but with one foot in life and one beyond, he seems very committed to the idea. Ingenious, eh what?"

Gable had had a similar idea earlier, but I didn't want to take the wind out of the big blowhard, so I agreed that it was truly inspired. Suddenly I spotted Humphrey Bogart at the far end of the studio, apparently giving a costume designer instructions about the pair of tights he was holding up. Somehow I still couldn't see him as Hamlet, in tights and soliloquies, but perhaps the tough old dog would find yet another dimension in that great work.

"And what about Bacall—have you been able to get her to play Ophelia?"

"On that point I'm afraid we failed. Simply too many difficulties. But I think Miss Monroe will make a splendid Ophelia. Indeed, she's particularly well experienced for the role."

"You mean to say Marilyn has played Ophelia before?"

"Oh, no, no. I am referring to Ophelia's end."

Good God! Producing a movie is a cold business. "I doubt she'd be interested. Besides, she's out of the country."

"Dead wrong on both counts. We got to her in New York on the plane to Monte Carlo and induced her to get off."

Since I hadn't seen them get off the plane, I supposed that for a while I had not been part of their world—that I had been in total contact with life. No wonder everything looked so grim.

"And when Mr. Bogart and I explained that we'd only meant to use Miss Bacall as her understudy in the role, essentially as a publicity stunt, she joined our production readily."

"You mean Marilyn is here at The Big House?"

"Quite! She's already rehearsing her lines, but as I said, the script needs work."

"Syd—may I call you Syd?—if your offer's still open, I'll take the job, but I still need the money for the brawl at the Century Plaza. I owe some money to a pal in New York."

"Agreed." He reached out, grabbed my hand, and nearly shook my arm out of the socket. "See Arthur and he will get you set up in an apartment in the residential wing and will show you to the cashier to be paid. Tomorrow morning you report directly to John Huston in the studio. Good luck! In the meantime, I must repair to the conference room. I have a production meeting scheduled with Messrs. Holzer and Bitzer." Sydney Greenstreet swung around like a side of beef and left.

A door with a star painted on it opened down in the studio, and Marilyn Monroe emerged, wearing a full-length, cream-colored dress, and with her hair done up in golden curls. My spirits danced at the sight of her, and I wondered if we could pick up where we had left off. But then I scolded myself for expecting too much. This was a new ball game, and I would have to take whatever I was dealt. Now Marilyn spotted me, and she stopped stone-still. Suddenly she began moving quickly in my direction, holding her dress off the dusty floor with one hand. I felt my legs carrying me down the stairs toward the concrete floor.

Marilyn and I were running toward each other over the planks, stepping over tools, but it might as well have been through a field of wild daisies. When we were just a few feet apart she leaped into the air, and feeling as if I, too, were lighter than air, I sprang up, and we seemed to meet at some time and place above it all, just as they do in shampoo commercials. In midflight we kissed, and when we finally settled back on the floor of the studio, Marilyn smiled so widely I could see every white tooth, and said softly, "At my apartment I have a package wrapped in brown paper that belongs to you. Why don't you drop over tonight, and I'll give it to you."

Obviously, I'd gone to heaven.